SCREAM SHOP
PICK YOUR PATH
Curse of Count Blood
By Tracey West

For my friend Dave, a memorable character in
every sense of the word—T.W.

For my sister Allison, who shows me every day
that through love we can persevere
through anything—B.D.

Copyright © 2004 by Tracey West. Illustrations copyright © 2004 by
Brian W. Dow. All rights reserved. Published by Grosset & Dunlap, a
division of Penguin Young Readers Group, 345 Hudson Street, New York,
New York 10014. GROSSET & DUNLAP is a trademark of Penguin
Group (USA) Inc. Printed in the U.S.A.

Library of Congress Control Number: 2004008301

ISBN 0-448-43556-X   10 9 8 7 6 5 4 3 2 1

S.CREAM SHOP

Curse of Count Blood

By Tracey West
Illustrated by Brian W. Dow

Grosset & Dunlap • New York

"Ivan, where are you off to this morning?" Ivan Melchik's grandmother didn't even look up from the pot she was stirring on the kitchen stove as her grandson headed toward the back door. It was only nine in the morning, but Nana was already cooking. She was always cooking something.

Ivan stopped. It was the first day of school vacation, and he knew exactly what he wanted to do. He just wasn't sure Nana would agree. His grandmother took care of Ivan during the day because both of his parents worked the night shift at the hospital.

"Just going downtown," Ivan said. It wasn't a lie—just not the whole truth. "I won't be long."

Nana looked up from her pot and stared at Ivan for a second. Her dark eyes seemed to glimmer in her pale, wrinkled face.

"Not the comic books again, Ivan," she said finally, shaking her head.

Ivan sighed. How did Nana always know?

"Please, Nana," Ivan begged. "I heard some kids in school talking about a store that sells weird old things. I'll just bet there's a box of old comic books there. Probably some rare stuff. It could be a gold mine!"

Collecting comic books was Ivan's passion. Old horror comic books were his favorites, with their shadowy illustrations of vampires, werewolves, and other monsters. He couldn't afford to buy the older books from regular comic-book dealers—they always jacked up the price way too high. Junk shops and garage sales were the best places to find the old books at cheap prices. If Sebastian Cream's Junk Shop was anything like he had heard, he was sure some treasures waited for him there.

Nana frowned. "All those scary stories! I'm surprised they don't give you nightmares."

"They don't!" Ivan said. "Please, Nana."

His grandmother gave in. "All right, Bubby," she said, and Ivan cringed at the nickname. Nana walked over and kissed Ivan on the forehead, and he cringed again. "Be careful."

"I will, Nana," Ivan promised. Then he hurried out the door before she could change her mind.

Ivan patted the folded piece of paper in his pocket as he headed down the street. He had printed out his updated comic-book list right after breakfast. It listed every issue of every comic book he had in his collection. He always took the list with him when he went hunting for new books. That way, he wouldn't buy the same book twice by mistake.

Ivan walked down several tree-lined streets

until he came to a sign for Wary Lane. Ivan turned left. The kids he had heard talking said it was near that shop that sold lampshades. Just Lampshades was just up ahead, all right. Ivan stopped and scanned the street.

And then he saw it, just across the street. Sebastian Cream's Junk Shop. Ivan ran to the store and peered inside the front window.

His own reflection peered back at him: a rather short, stout body; a mop of black hair; and glasses with very thick frames. Past his reflection, the items in the window looked promising. A large oil painting of a sailing ship leaned against a chair covered in red velvet. A stuffed shark mounted on a plaque stared at an old ventriloquist's dummy. The rest of the display was cluttered with stacks of old books, glass bottles, and other items.

Ivan pushed open the front door, his heart beating quickly. He was going to find something good here—he could just feel it. Inside the shop, shelves and tables held more unusual items. Ivan spotted a counter in the back. A man who looked like he must be the shopkeeper stood behind it. He was talking to a boy and girl Ivan's age. Ivan ignored them and addressed the shopkeeper.

"Excuse me," he asked. "Do you sell old comic books here?"

The boy and the girl walked out, leaving Ivan

alone with the shopkeeper. The man had a round body and white hair. Green eyes peered out behind wire-rimmed glasses. He smiled at Ivan.

"My name is Sebastian Cream," he said. "May I help you?"

Hadn't the man heard him? Ivan repeated his question. "I was just wondering if you had any old comic books lying around."

Mr. Cream shook his head. "I'm afraid I don't," he said. "Perhaps there's something else in the store you might like."

Ivan felt crushed. "No thanks," he muttered. He turned to leave.

Then something caught his eye.

Something silver glittered in a small glass case on the counter. Ivan leaned closer.

It was a small glass vial, filled with what looked like gray dust. A cork kept the dust inside the vial. But what interested Ivan was the silver emblem wrapped around the vial. Engraved in the silver was a bat flying across the moon.

"That looks like the symbol of Count Blood," Ivan said excitedly.

Count Blood was one of Ivan's favorite comic-book characters. Even though he was a vampire, he used his vampire powers to fight against evil. There had been 113 issues of *Count Blood* published in the 1970s, and Ivan had almost all of them in his collection.

Mr. Cream took the vial out of the case and handed it to Ivan, who inspected it more closely. It was the symbol of Count Blood, all right. *It must be some kind of rare promotional item*, he thought— maybe something you could send away for in the back of the comic book.

"How much?" Ivan asked.

Mr. Cream named a price, and Ivan carefully counted out the money from his pocket. Every penny he earned from his allowance and from recycling bottles and cans went toward his comic-book collection.

The shop owner put the vial in a bag and handed it to Ivan, smiling. "An interesting item for an interesting boy," he said.

"Uh, thanks," Ivan replied. Then he left the shop, clutching his prize.

Ivan wanted to get out his comic books right away, to see if he could find any mention of the vial, but Nana had other plans for him. She kept Ivan busy dusting the furniture and helping with the laundry. Then his parents came home from work, and they all ate the huge dinner that Nana had cooked. As soon as Ivan swallowed his last bite, he ran upstairs.

Ivan kept his comic books alphabetized in special cardboard boxes. They took up almost one whole wall in his room. He took out the box carefully labeled "Ce-Co," and began to thumb through the *Count Blood* comic books.

Ivan lost track of the time as he thumbed through the books, stopping to re-read the stories again. Count Blood was so amazing! Ivan loved his costume: a black cape, lined in red, with a high collar. Underneath he wore a white shirt, black jacket, and red vest. He had a long, pale face, and his black hair was slicked back and shiny. Around his neck he wore the medallion with the symbol of the bat flying across the moon.

At some point, Ivan's parents opened the door and said good night, and Ivan mumbled good night back to them and kept reading. Finally, he yawned. He hadn't found anything advertising the vial, but he still had more comic books to look through. Before he stood up, he turned the vial in his fingers, examining it.

"Ow!" Ivan cried suddenly. The edge of the metal emblem was unexpectedly sharp. It sliced through his index finger. A small river of blood immediately coursed down his hand.

Ivan stuck his finger in his mouth to try to stop the bleeding. To his dismay, he saw that some of the blood had stained the cork. A few drops had seeped through into the vial.

"Rats!" Ivan exclaimed. If the vial really was a

rare item, he had just ruined its value.

Suddenly, Ivan felt a tingling in his hand. The vial felt red hot. Ivan threw it to the floor without thinking.

Bam! There was a small explosion as the vial burst into pieces. Gray smoke filled the room. Ivan watched, shocked, as a large shape began to form inside the smoke.

The smoke cleared, and a tall man in a black suit and cape stood there. Two long, sharp fangs extended from his mouth. He immediately lunged at Ivan, baring his fangs.

Startled, Ivan grabbed the nearest thing he could find—his desk chair. He held it in front of him like a lion tamer facing a lion.

"G-g-g-go away!" Ivan cried, his heart pounding in his chest.

A confused look crossed the man's face. He stopped, and then looked around the room.

"I am very sorry," he said in a thick accent. "Allow me to introduce myself. I am Count Blood."

"Count Blood?" The man looked like Count Blood, all right. But what was he doing here? It was like something out of, well, a comic book. Ivan slowly lowered his chair.

"I vill not harm you," the vampire said. "But I must ask you: Ven is the next sunrise? I must seek shelter before the sun rises."

Ivan couldn't speak. Count Blood was standing before him in the flesh. A real live vampire. He must be dreaming.

He pinched himself. He thought that was what people did when they were seeing things? But all he did was make his arm hurt.

"I'm . . . not sure," Ivan said. It was true. He looked at his digital clock, which read 4:00 a.m. He had no idea what time the sun rose. For all he knew, it could be soon.

"Then you must help me," Count Blood said. "Give me shelter somevhere safe. Your basement, perhaps. Then I vill visit you again tomorrow evening."

Ivan didn't know what to say. Count Blood, the vampire superhero, was asking for his help. That was pretty cool. Then again, Count Blood was still a vampire—and he had attacked Ivan once already. Maybe stashing a blood-sucking creature of the night in his basement wasn't such a great idea.

If Ivan lets Count Blood stay, go to page 13.

If Ivan asks Count Blood to leave, go to page 62.

Continued from page 12

Ivan decided not to worry. In all the issues of *Count Blood* he had read, the vampire had never bitten a human. And there was so much he wanted to ask Count Blood! It was too good an opportunity to miss.

"Sure you can stay in our basement," Ivan said.

"That is very kind of you," said Count Blood. "Perhaps ve should make haste and go there now."

Ivan put a finger to his lips and motioned for Count Blood to follow him. The two walked silently down the hallway, which was lit by a night-light. They crept down the stairs and then Ivan led the vampire through the kitchen to the base-ment door.

The basement held the Melchiks' washer and dryer, along with boxes of holiday decorations, lawn chairs, and other seasonal items.

"We, uh, don't have a coffin or anything," Ivan said apologetically.

"That is not necessary," Count Blood said. "I just need protection from the sunlight."

"No windows down here," Ivan said. "You should be safe."

The vampire unfolded one of the lawn chairs. He lay on his back, then crossed his hands on his chest.

"Very comfortable," he said. "Be sure to vake me before the sun goes down. I have very important vork to do!"

Ivan nodded. "Sure," he said. "Good night."

Ivan quietly walked back upstairs to his room. He'd have to keep guard over the basement tomorrow. It shouldn't be too hard—his parents would be at work. He'd just have to stay close to Nana to make sure she didn't go down there for any reason.

Ivan set his alarm for six. He sprang out of bed as soon as it rang. Then he ran downstairs and found Nana, fully dressed, cooking on the stove.

"My, you're up early," she said, smiling.

Ivan tried not to yawn. "Am I?" he said casually.

"Sit down and I'll make you breakfast," Nana said.

Everything seemed fine. After a huge breakfast of eggs, sausages, and blintzes, Ivan settled at the kitchen table with his Count Blood comic books so he could keep an eye on the basement door. Nana scoffed at the comics at first, but seemed pleased that Ivan wanted to spend the day with her. As Nana cooked, Ivan read more of Count Blood's adventures.

One of the story lines fascinated him. Even though he didn't have every single issue, he was still able to follow the story: A young vampire named Fang led a vampire war against Count Blood and his clan. Fang thought Count Blood gave vampires a bad name by being a good guy. In the last issue Ivan had, Fang staked Count Blood in the heart, turning him to dust.

Although reading the comics was fun, Ivan thought the day would never end. Finally, a few minutes after Ivan and his family finished eating supper, the sun set. Ivan waited until Nana, Mom, and Dad were in the living room watching TV. Then he went down into the basement.

The bottom step creaked as Ivan's foot hit it, and Count Blood immediately sat upright, his dark eyes glittering. Ivan nearly jumped out of his skin.

"Has the sun set?" the vampire asked.

Ivan nodded. "About five minutes ago."

"Good." Count Blood stood up. "I must go vhile there is time. I have much to do."

"Wait!" Ivan cried. "I mean, where are you going?" He had so many questions he wanted to ask.

The count studied Ivan's face. "You have been a good host," he said finally. "Very vell. I vill tell you. I must return to my old crypt. There, I vill find the tools I need to track my greatest enemy. The vampire who turned me to dust."

"Fang?" Ivan asked, his eyes wide.

"How did you know that?" Count Blood asked.

"It's in the comic book," Ivan explained.

Count Blood sighed. "Ah, that silly book. Yes, it is true. I must find Fang and destroy him for vat he did to me."

"Can I come?" Ivan blurted out, although as soon as he said it he knew it sounded crazy.

Count Blood looked thoughtful. "You may come to my crypt vith me," he said. "You showed bravery last night ven I first appeared to you, and there may be danger ahead. But I vill not take you to meet Fang. That vould be foolish."

Ivan felt relieved. "Fine," he said. "And thanks."

So Ivan made sure the coast was clear. He told his parents he was going to the library, then he snuck Count Blood out the back door. It was already dark out, and Ivan was grateful. If any-one spotted him walking with the strange, caped man, he'd have a lot of explaining to do.

Count Blood led Ivan through the streets of Bleaktown to Mount Hope Cemetery, the largest cemetery in town. They passed through the cemetery gates. Finally, they stopped in front of a small stone crypt. It was about the size of a garden shed, but it was made of stone that was now crumbling and discolored by age and rain.

"Velcome to my home," Count Blood said, and he pushed on the heavy stone door.

"What do we have here? Fresh meat!"

A tall, musclebound vampire stood behind the door. Ivan could tell he was a vampire because his wide mouth was open, revealing two long fangs. His bulging arms were covered with tattoos of skulls and bats.

The vampire stepped out of the shadows, and Ivan could see at least three more vampires behind him.

A red fire burned in Count Blood's eyes. He spread out his cape and glared at the vampires.

"How dare you invade my home?" he asked in a voice that sounded like rumbling thunder. The vampires exchanged nervous glances.

"Ivan, run!" Count Blood demanded in a voice Ivan dared not refuse. "I vill take care of these trespassers."

Ivan looked around. The main gate they had come through seemed to be miles away. There was an open gate nearby, but Ivan had no idea where it led.

If Ivan runs toward the nearest gate, go to page 29.

If Ivan runs back to the main gate, go to page 20.

Continued from page 47

Ivan pushed the door shut behind him, then took the left-hand tunnel. He could barely see in the darkness.

He didn't get far before he came to a wall, set with flat stones the size of his hand. The passage-way was blocked.

"Rats!" Ivan cried. He smacked his hand against one of the stones.

Incredibly, the wall began to slide to the side. Ivan stepped inside. As his eyes adjusted to the darkness, he could see he was in a small chamber of some kind. A round pillar rose up from the floor in the center of the chamber. And something on top of the pillar glittered in the dim light.

Ivan cautiously moved closer. The glittering object looked round, and about the same size as Count Blood's medallion.

Then Ivan remembered the small penlight he always carried on his key chain. Ivan unhooked the key chain from his belt and shone the light on the object.

Ivan gasped. It looked just like Count Blood's medallion. He picked it up to examine it closer and saw it was hanging from a thick silver chain.

Then Ivan heard footsteps coming down the tunnel. Fang—or his crew—must have figured out he had escaped through the hidden door!

Ivan shone the penlight around the chamber. There was no way out.

Then he looked at the medallion in his hand, and a thought crossed his mind.

Count Blood's medallion gave *him* special powers. Maybe the medallion would do the same for Ivan. He could use any extra help he could get.

Ivan started to put the medallion around his neck, then hesitated. What if this medallion had different powers—evil powers? Ivan wasn't so sure he should mess with something he didn't fully understand.

If Ivan puts on the medallion, go to page 60.

If Ivan doesn't put on the medallion, go to page 89.

Continued from page 17

Ivan felt safer running for the main gate, so he zipped behind Count Blood and began to zigzag through the gravestones.

He didn't get far before he felt a strong hand on his shoulder. He turned to see the tattooed vampire glaring at him.

"I'm taking you back to Fang," he growled. Then he grabbed the front of Ivan's T-shirt and lifted him off the ground.

Ivan craned his neck to see what had happened to Count Blood. The superhero was tossing one of the vampires over his head. The rest of the vampires were sprawled on the ground around him. If they had tried to fight Count Blood, then they had lost.

"Count Blood!" Ivan yelled, as the vampire dragged him away.

Count Blood came sweeping across the cemetery, almost as though he were flying. He pulled the big vampire off Ivan.

The tattooed vampire struggled to get out of Count Blood's grasp. He grabbed onto the medallion that hung around the count's neck. At the same time, Count Blood slammed the tattooed vampire onto a nearby tombstone. Ivan saw the medallion fly out of the vampire's hands, and he ran to grab it.

"Thanks, Count," Ivan said, casting a glance at the tattooed vampire. He seemed to be out cold. "I think these guys are with Fang. That big one said—"

The look in Count Blood's eyes stopped him in his tracks. It could only be described as evil, Ivan thought. The count slowly moved toward Ivan.

"I am very hungry, Ivan," he said. "I have not eaten in such a long time."

Ivan ran. He had no idea where he was going, or how he would escape from a vampire who could fly. He just knew he didn't want to get eaten.

When Ivan reached the cemetery gates, he snuck a look behind him. To his relief, he saw Count Blood hadn't followed him. Oddly, the count was shaking the hand of the tattooed vampire.

Ivan ran all the way home, his mind racing.

Something's wrong with Count Blood. He's evil now or something.

And he knows where I live.

As soon as Ivan got home, he grabbed all of the garlic heads he could find in the wire basket in Nana's kitchen. He broke up the cloves and then ran around the house, scattering garlic everywhere.

Ivan made himself a necklace out of the garlic that was left and went upstairs to his bedroom. He took his desk chair and faced it toward his window.

He'd stay awake all night if he had to. He had to protect his family from Count Blood.

Ivan stared out of the window for an hour and his eyes began to droop. He decided to look through his Count Blood comic-book collection to see if there was anything there that might help him.

The first thing that jumped out at Ivan was the name on the inside cover: Dave Coburn, writer and penciler.

Dave Coburn must have known the real Count Blood, Ivan realized. *How else could he have written all of those stories?* Excited, he ran to his desk and pulled out an envelope in his top drawer.

Last year, Ivan had written a fan letter to Dave Coburn. After a few months, Coburn had written back. Ivan looked at the envelope. The return address said Springfield—just a short ride away from Bleaktown.

Ivan fell asleep halfway through his watch that night, but he was relieved to see that his family was safe. After breakfast, he hopped on a bus to Springfield and found Dave Coburn's address.

He ended up in front of a small white house with a neat lawn. Ivan walked to the front door and rang the bell.

The door opened to reveal a medium-sized, stocky man with bushy brown hair. He wore jeans, slippers, and a Bugs Bunny T-shirt.

"I don't need any cookies," he said grumpily.

"Dave Coburn?" Ivan asked nervously.

"That's me."

"It's about Count Blood—" Ivan began.

Coburn started to close the door. "Forget it, kid. That part of my life is over."

Ivan quickly pulled the medallion out of his pocket and pushed it through the crack in the door. "But I know he's real! And he's in trouble."

Coburn sighed, raised an eyebrow, and opened the door.

"Come on in," he said.

He led Ivan into a neat living room and motioned for him to sit on the couch. As soon as Ivan did, Coburn took the medallion from him.

"Where did you get this?" he asked suspiciously.

Ivan launched into his story, starting with how he had bought the vial and ending with the fight in the cemetery.

"It's like Count Blood went all evil or something," Ivan said.

Coburn nodded. "The medallion is what keeps his vampire urges under control. Without it, he's just a regular evil vampire."

"But he knows where I live," Ivan said, panicking. "He'll come after me!"

"That's your problem, kid," Coburn said. "I

washed my hands of Count Blood a long time ago. After he went and got himself dusted by Fang, they ended the comic book. I couldn't think of anything else to write. Now I make a living painting murals in seafood restaurants. If I have to paint one more lobster, I'm going to go nuts! I don't want anything to do with Blood." Coburn stood up. "Sorry I can't help you."

Ivan thought quickly. "You have to help me. The count might come after you. After all, he knows where *you* live, too."

Coburn scowled. "I guess you're right," he said, sitting down again. "Okay. There are a few things you can do. But after this conversation, you're on your own, kid. Got it?"

"Fine," Ivan said. The comic-book creator wasn't the friendliest guy, but at least he was helping.

"Number one," said Coburn. "Find out where Count Blood sleeps during the day. Then slip the medallion back on him while he's asleep."

"He was sleeping in my basement," Ivan said.

"He's probably back in his headquarters," Coburn said.

"You mean in the cemetery?" Ivan asked.

The artist shook his head. "That's not his main hangout. His real headquarters was under the Bleaktown Historical Society. I had to change it for the comic book so no one would find out."

Ivan frowned. "That sounds dangerous. What if he wakes up?"

"There's another way to go," Coburn said. "Remember issue number fifty-seven? Count Blood's medallion fell off, and Dr. Mystic from the League of Superheroes performed a spell to make him good again. It worked until they were able to find the medallion. If you did the spell, you wouldn't have to go near Count Blood or his coffin."

Ivan thought about what to do. He'd have to try something—but he didn't want to do it alone.

"Listen," Ivan said. "Why don't you help me? If Count Blood becomes a hero again, you can write more comics about him. Then you'd never have to paint another lobster."

Coburn scratched his chin thoughtfully. "You've got a point there," he said. "All right. What do you want to do?"

If Ivan and Dave decide to go to Count Blood's coffin, go to page 69.

If Ivan and Dave try Dr. Mystic's spell, go to page 124.

"Let's try, '*strength of earth*,'" Ivan said quickly.
Coburn nodded. They began the spell again.
"Depth of sea.
Strength of earth.
Light of moon.
Power of sun.
May thy powers be undone."
Once again, they said the words three times—
but faster, this time, because Fang had begun to
walk around the cemetery, sniffing around. He
stopped in front of their clump of bushes just as
they finished saying the last word.

At that exact moment, Ivan saw Fang's body
begin to shimmer faintly. A duplicate of Fang
stepped out of its body—only this Fang looked
as though it were made of mist. Ghost-like, just
as Coburn had said. Then the ghostly figure
evaporated.

"Not again!" Fang wailed.

"I am afraid so," said Count Blood. "But this
time, I vill fight you."

Fang gasped. Count Blood stood in the center
of the cemetery as though he had appeared out of
nowhere. Ivan saw that the tough-looking biker
vampires didn't look so tough anymore. They
each took a few steps back.

Fang gathered his courage. "I dusted you once before, Blood," he growled. "And I'll do it again!"

Fang lunged at Count Blood. He had his hands raised. Ivan remembered that in the comic book, Fang could shoot red lightning bolts from his fingers.

But nothing came out. Fang scowled and kept going, his hands balled into fists now.

He aimed a powerful blow at Count Blood's chest. Normally, a blow like that from a vampire as strong as Fang would send anyone—even Count Blood—flying. But Count Blood stood firm.

Suddenly, a white light shot out of Count Blood's medallion. The light enveloped Fang. He struggled to escape from it, but couldn't.

"Farevell, Fang," Count Blood said.

"Noooooo!" Fang cried.

In the next instant, the ball of light exploded. Fang vanished in a blaze of white heat.

Count Blood stared at the motorcycle vampires.

"Leave this place," he said. "Or you vill be next."

The vampires acted quickly. They hopped on their bikes and roared off into the night.

Ivan and Coburn emerged from the bushes.

"Wow!" Ivan said. "That was great!"

"You're back in action, Count," Coburn said, slapping the vampire on the back.

"I guess I am," said the vampire. "It feels good."

They drove back to Coburn's house. He poured another glass of pig's blood for the count and handed Ivan a cup of hot chocolate. "We've got to get you home soon, kid," he said. "But we should celebrate first."

"So what will you do now?" Ivan asked Count Blood.

"I vould like to fight crime again," Count Blood said. "That is, if you vill help me, Ivan."

Ivan couldn't believe it. Help Count Blood, a real live superhero? "Of course!" Ivan replied.

"Hey, you wouldn't mind if I started drawing a comic book about you again, would you?" Coburn asked.

"Of course not," Count Blood said. "You alvays did capture me very vell."

Ivan smiled. Fang was defeated. Count Blood was back in business—and Ivan was going to help him. And Dave Coburn was going to revive the Count Blood comic book.

"I'd say this is a pretty happy ending!" Ivan remarked.

THE END

The large vampire sprang forward, and Ivan charged toward the nearest gate. He heard a whooshing sound behind him and turned to look. Count Blood was gone; in his place, a black bat flapped its wings.

The vampires stopped and stared. "It really is Count Blood!" the tattooed vampire cried. "Fang's got to hear about this!" Then he and the other vampires turned and took off in the opposite direction.

Ivan kept running. He didn't stop until he had passed through the cemetery gates and ran down several streets until the cemetery was no longer in view. As he leaned against a tree, panting, the black bat flew up. It transformed into Count Blood before his eyes.

"That one guy said something about Fang," Ivan said. "Do you think they work for him?"

"Undoubtedly," the count replied. "I should like to know vat they vere doink in my crypt."

The boy and the vampire walked back down the dark streets toward Ivan's house.

"What do you think Fang will do once he hears you're alive—I mean, undead, again?" Ivan asked.

"He vill come looking for me, of course," Count Blood said. "Perhaps it is not safe for me to return to your home, Ivan."

Ivan thought about it. "I don't think they're

following us. We should be safe for another day. And maybe I could go back to the crypt during the day to look for those tools for you."

"You should be safe during the day," Count Blood said. "That is a very good idea, Ivan. You are very smart for such a young man."

Ivan could feel his cheeks blush. It felt cool to be helping a real-life superhero like Count Blood.

Back at Ivan's house, Ivan snuck Count Blood back into the basement. They spent some time hiding Count Blood's lawn chair from sight in case Nana came into the basement the next day. Soon Ivan began to yawn.

"You are not a creature of the night, like me," Count Blood said. "Get some rest, Ivan. I have much thinking to do."

The next morning, Ivan headed back to the cemetery. He clutched a head of garlic in one hand and a cross made of two sticks in the other, just in case. When he arrived, he saw that the door to Count Blood's crypt was still open.

"Hello?" Ivan called out cautiously.

There was no reply, and Ivan stepped inside. The stone room was just as Count Blood had described it, and to Ivan's relief, it was empty.

The count had told him that he would find an old metal box behind a secret stone panel in the back wall. Ivan counted seven stones up and seven stones in and then pushed gently.

The stone receded, revealing a small cubbyhole. The metal box was there, but its lock had been broken open. And it was empty.

Ivan told Count Blood of his findings as soon as the sun went down.

"Very interesting," Count Blood said. "Fang must have the key to my old headquarters. I vonder if he is staying there."

"I thought the crypt was your headquarters," Ivan said.

"Just a front," Count Blood said. "For years, my followers and I lived in a secret underground chamber beneath the Bleaktown Historical Society. Some of my deepest secrets are hidden there. I just hope Fang has not found them."

"We should go there," Ivan suggested. "Find out what he's up to."

"That could be too dangerous," Count Blood said. "I have no idea how many minions Fang has in his control. Perhaps I could lure him out of hiding and confront him, one on one."

"Do you think he'd really do that?" Ivan asked.

If Ivan and Count Blood check out the old hideout, go to page 55.

If Ivan and Count Blood decide to issue a challenge to Fang, go to page 43.

Continued from page 65

Ivan decided to tell Sasha the truth. Count Blood was a superhero, after all. Even if Sasha was lying about him being a bad guy, what could one woman do against a super-hero vampire?

"He said he had a crypt at Mount Hope Cemetery," Ivan said. "That's all I know."

Sasha studied Ivan's face, as though she were trying to determine if he was lying. Finally she nodded, satisfied.

"Thanks," she said. Then she turned and walked down the steps.

Ivan's nana turned the corner seconds later. She frowned at Sasha and then ran up to Ivan.

"Who was that woman?" Nana asked. "Did you invite her into the house?"

Ivan thought quickly. "She was selling magazine subscriptions," he said. "I told her we didn't want any."

"Good. But you should not have opened the door," Nana scolded.

Nana finished the soup a little while later, and she and Ivan sat at the kitchen table, eating in silence. Ivan kept thinking about Sasha.

Had he done the right thing? There was something about Sasha he just didn't like. If Count Blood got hurt because of him, he'd never forgive himself.

"Nana, can I take a walk after lunch?" Ivan asked. "It's a nice day out, and I'm a growing boy. I need fresh air."

"Of course," Nana agreed. "You're right. And you can help me clean the closet when you get back."

Ivan slurped the last of his soup and ran upstairs to get his backpack. He stuffed in a few issues of *Count Blood* and a pair of binoculars he used for bird-watching. Then he headed outside.

The largest cemetery in Bleaktown, Mount Hope, was a low, green hill dotted with tombstones, stone crypts, and statues. Ivan walked through the iron gates and then took the binoculars out of his backpack. He didn't want Sasha to know he was looking for her, if he could help it.

Ivan scanned the cemetery. He knew from visiting his grandfather's grave that the oldest graves were in the back, farthest from the gate. Ivan focused the binoculars on the area.

A figure in black passed across his line of sight. Ivan lowered the binoculars. It looked like Sasha, all right.

He carefully made his way through the cemetery, moving from tree to tree so he wouldn't be seen as easily. Finally he found the perfect viewing spot: a clump of bushes about twenty feet away from Sasha. Ivan crouched down behind them and looked through his binoculars again.

Sasha was standing in front of a small stone crypt. It was about the size of a garden shed, but it was made of stone that was now crumbling and discolored by age and rain. She wore a satisfied look on her face.

Sasha set a large black case on the ground and opened it up. She took out a tool that looked like some kind of electric saw. Ivan watched as she walked all around the perimeter of the crypt, pressing the tool against the stone. It took Ivan a few minutes to realize what she was doing— drilling round holes all around the crypt.

Holes? Ivan wondered. *Why would she do that?*

Sasha stopped and looked up at the sun, grinning.

She's letting sunlight into the crypt, Ivan realized. Sunlight was deadly to vampires.

Sasha walked inside the crypt, and Ivan heard a scream. Sasha left the crypt, looked both ways, and then took off running.

When Sasha had left, Ivan ran inside the crypt. Bright sunlight streamed in through the holes. A coffin sat on a platform in the middle of the crypt, its lid wide open. Gray smoke billowed from the open coffin.

Ivan came closer, afraid of what he might see. But he had to look.

Count Blood lay in the coffin. Smoke poured

from his skin.

"Count Blood!" Ivan cried. "I'll get you out of here."

"It is too late for me, Ivan," he croaked in a dry voice. "Sasha has been here. She hates all vampires. Even those of us who do no harm."

At that moment, Ivan knew he had done the wrong thing by telling Sasha how to find Count Blood. But it was too late. The smoke billowed harder, and in the next instant, Count Blood turned to dust.

"Nooooo!" Ivan screamed.

He tried to think. Maybe it wasn't too late. Ivan had revived Count Blood once before. Maybe he could do it again.

Ivan dug in his pocket and found a round pin with the Captain Amazing logo on it—another of his favorite comics. He pricked his finger with the sharp end of the pin and let a few drops of blood fall into the dust in the coffin.

Nothing happened.

Ivan frowned. Then he remembered the vial.

Maybe the vial has something to do with reviving the count, Ivan guessed. He'd have to get another one. And he knew just where to look.

Go to page 93.

Continued from page 88

Ivan remembered Coburn's awesome fight with Count Blood and decided he could trust him.

"All right," he said. "We'll go straight back to Count Blood's coffin. But what do we do when we get there?"

"Let's talk in the car," Coburn said. "If we want the advantage, we've got to beat Fang there."

They discussed the plan as Coburn drove to the historical society. If they beat Fang there, they would hide in the bushes bordering the tiny cemetery. As soon as Fang showed up, Coburn and Ivan would begin reciting the incantation.

"Vonce ve see the spell take effect, I vill attack Fang," Count Blood said.

"How will we know if it works?" Ivan asked.

"Don't you remember?" Coburn said. "When Dr. Mystic did it to Fang, you could see the power leaving Fang. It was like a ghost of Fang stepped out of him. I remember drawing it. Totally cool."

The image popped into Ivan's mind as Coburn described it. "I remember!" he said excitedly. "Man, I hope it works."

Coburn pulled in front of the Bleaktown Historical Society a few minutes later. They all got out of the car and cautiously walked to the back of the building.

There was no sign of Fang or his crew. Ivan scanned the tiny cemetery until he found a clump of bushes big enough to hide him and Coburn. He and Dave crouched down behind the leafy branches. Count Blood walked to the tall tombstone and placed his hand on it. He began to sink into the ground.

"I vill vait down here," he said. "It vill help me to catch Fang by surprise. I vill be able to hear everything that happens. Good luck, my friends."

Count Blood disappeared inside the tunnels. The piece of earth rose up, so that the cemetery once again looked normal.

Coburn and Ivan waited in silence, not daring to speak. Finally Ivan spoke in a whisper.

"Maybe he's not coming," Ivan whispered.

"Nah, Fang's always a little bit late," Coburn whispered back. "He hates to get out of bed."

Suddenly, a bright light flooded the yard, and the sound of roaring motors filled their ears. Through spaces in the bushes, Ivan saw at least ten motorcycles ride behind the historical society.

Each motorcycle was topped by a man in a black leather jacket. The same patch adorned the right sleeve of each of the jackets—a neon yellow skull. Ivan recognized the symbol from the *Count*

Blood comic book. It belonged to Fang.

The motorcycles formed a circle around the graveyard. They came to a stop and turned off their lights. One of the riders stepped off his bike and into the center. Ivan saw he had a long, thin face, scraggly blond hair, and a beard. Underneath his jacket he wore a red T-shirt emblazoned with the same yellow skull.

It was Fang. Ivan would recognize that face anywhere. It struck him what a good artist Dave Coburn was. He had captured Count Blood and Fang on paper perfectly.

"Blood said he'd meet us here," Fang said. He turned to one of the bikers, who Ivan recognized as the tattooed vampire from the cemetery. "You sure he's on our side?"

"Sure," the vampire answered. "I tore off his medallion. And he tried to bite a kid."

"He'd better show up soon," Fang scowled. "High-and-mighty vamp. Thinks he can keep Fang waiting? He'd better think again."

"Okay," Coburn whispered while Fang was talking. "Let's do it. Three times, like Dr. Mystic did."

Ivan and Coburn recited the spell together.

Depth of sea.
Strength of rock.
Light of moon.
Power of sun.

May thy powers be undone."

They whispered the words three times. Then they waited.

Nothing happened.

"It's not working," Ivan hissed.

Coburn frowned. "I'm sure those were the words."

"I don't think so," Ivan said. "The second line doesn't feel right. I think it was strength of earth. Or maybe force of rock. I can't remember."

"Well try!" Coburn said impatiently.

Fang stopped talking and sniffed the air. "Did you hear something?" he asked.

Coburn whispered in Ivan's ear. "Make it fast, kid. We've got to try again."

If Ivan goes with "Strength of earth," go to page 26.

If Ivan goes with "Force of rock," go to page 72.

Ivan turned and ran. This was all Coburn's fault, anyway.

But then he felt a cold hand on his arm. "So you have my medallion, do you?" Count Blood stared at him menacingly.

Then Blood fell forward. Coburn had tackled him from behind. He stepped on Count Blood's back, holding him down.

"Quick, kid," he said. "Give it to me!"

Ivan tossed him the medallion. Coburn reached down to put it on the count's neck . . .

The vampire pushed back with tremendous force. Coburn went flying backward, slamming into the coffin. Count Blood towered over Ivan, holding his cape out wide.

"You vill pay for this, Ivan," the count said. "You vill pay!"

Ivan found himself staring into the vampire's eyes, which had turned the color of blood. His head began to feel fuzzy. The last thing he remembered was Count Blood's eyes getting closer . . . and closer . . .

Ivan woke up. He was someplace dark, but it wasn't Count Blood's chamber. He slowly sat up and looked around.

He was in a basement. Paneling covered the

walls, and he could make out a washer and dryer, and a foosball table. It wasn't his basement, though.

Then he looked down. He was dressed in a black suit with a cape around his shoulders. Count Blood's medallion dangled around his neck. And that wasn't all.

He was sitting in a coffin!

"Aaaaah!" Ivan screamed. "What's going on?"

As he talked, he noticed that his mouth felt strange—like it was filled with extra teeth or something.

At that moment, Dave Coburn came down the basement stairs. His face was covered with scratches and bruises.

"Hey, you're awake," he said.

"What happened?" Ivan asked. "The last thing I remember, Count Blood was coming after me."

Coburn took a small mirror out of his pocket. He handed it to Ivan.

"You got bit, kid."

Ivan got a sick feeling in his stomach. He held the mirror up to his neck and saw two small, red puncture wounds. Then he opened his mouth and saw two long fangs gleaming there.

"Am I a . . . a . . ." Ivan wasn't sure he wanted the answer.

"I tried to save you, kid," Coburn said. "But when I slammed into the coffin, it knocked me out. By the time I woke up, it was too late to save you. I fought Blood. Hurt him bad. Then I grabbed you and got out of there."

"But I can't be a vampire!" Ivan cried, panic rising in his voice. "I don't want to hurt anybody!"

"As long as you wear that medallion, you'll be fine," Coburn reminded him. But Ivan could tell from the sound of his voice that Coburn felt sorry for him.

Then Coburn brightened. "You know, it might not be so bad. No offense, kid, but I'll bet you weren't the most popular guy in school before this, right?"

"No," Ivan admitted.

"Well, now you get to be a superhero!" Coburn said. "I could do another comic book: *Count Melchik, Boy Vampire*. Got a nice ring, doesn't it?"

Ivan had to admit that it did. The more he thought about it, the better he felt. He never liked the sun much, anyway. It always gave him a rash.

"Very vell," said Ivan. He climbed out of the coffin. He opened his cape and tried to look menacing. "How's this for a cover pose?"

Coburn smiled. "Not bad, kid. Not bad!"

THE END

"I think he might," Count Blood said. "Fang is very proud. He would not refuse a challenge."

Count Blood and Ivan came up with a plan. The next day, Ivan would return to the cemetery with a note for Fang, issuing the challenge from Count Blood. If Fang accepted, he would meet the count in the cemetery at midnight.

Ivan got some paper for the count, who wrote the letter to Fang and then sealed it in an envelope. He handed the letter to Ivan.

Ivan slept with the letter under his pillow, to keep it safe. The next morning, Nana kept Ivan busy with chores and then fed him a big lunch of chicken and potatoes. It was late afternoon by the time Ivan headed to the cemetery again.

Count Blood had said to leave the letter inside the door of his old crypt. Before Ivan opened the door, he checked his pockets to make sure he still had the garlic and the cross. Then he took a deep breath. Even though the sun was shining, it creeped him out to be back at the crypt again.

Ivan stepped inside, into the darkness. He took the letter out of his pocket and looked for some way to leave it so that Fang's minions got it. The quicker he left the crypt, the happier he'd be.

"Aaaaiiiieeeeeeeeee!"

A high-pitched scream rang through the crypt. Ivan nearly jumped out of his skin. On instinct, he turned around.

A young, blonde-haired woman came running toward him. She looked terrified.

"Help!" she cried. "Something back there took my friend! Some kind of monster!"

Ivan quickly pulled out the garlic and cross, suspicious. He held them both in front of his face.

"Get back, vampire!" he yelled.

The woman began to sob. "I don't know what you're talking about! My friend needs help. Please!"

Ivan hesitated. The woman didn't look like a vampire. And she didn't seem bothered by the garlic or the cross.

If Count Blood were here, he would help her, Ivan thought. He put down his hands and nodded.

"Follow me!" the woman said. "My name's Rose," she explained. "My friend and I came to the cemetery on a dare. The door to the crypt was open, so we walked in. Then this monster guy with fangs grabbed Susie and took her somewhere down here!"

"How far did they go?" Ivan asked. It seemed like they had walked for a mile.

"Almost there," Rose said. They reached another turn, and Rose stopped.

"Can I have that stuff?" Rose asked, motioning toward the garlic and cross. "It would make me feel safer."

"Sure," Ivan said, and Rose gave him a big smile as he handed them over.

They turned the corner—and found themselves face to face with a group of vampires! The tattooed vampire stood in front of the group.

"Rose, run!" Ivan cried.

But Rose just smiled again. "Oh, I'm fine," she said. She threw the garlic and cross back down the tunnel. Then she walked over and linked arms with the tattooed vampire. "Is this the right kid?" she asked.

The tattooed vampire nodded. "That's him," he said. "Let's bring him to Fang."

Two tough-looking vampires grabbed Ivan by the arms and dragged him away. Ivan quickly realized he had been tricked.

"Hey, you said you weren't a vampire!" Ivan called out to Rose.

Rose shrugged. "I'm not. I just like to hang out with them."

Ivan, you're so stupid, he scolded himself. His mind raced. What did the vampires want with him? Probably dinner. He tried not to panic.

The vampires took him through a doorway and then pushed him inside. Ivan slowly looked around.

Rock posters covered the walls. The stone floor was littered with clothes, CDs, and empty snack bags. In the center of the room was a gray, stone coffin resting on a stone platform.

Suddenly, a man sat up in the coffin. He had a long, thin face, scraggly blond hair and beard, and wire-rimmed glasses. He wore a red T-shirt emblazoned with a neon yellow skull.

"Fang?" Ivan whispered. He recognized him from the comic book.

"So you're the kid hanging with Blood," Fang stated. "You look like a real wimp. Couldn't Blood get a better sidekick than you?"

Fang jumped out of his coffin and stuck his face in Ivan's. Ivan could see two long, yellowed fangs in his mouth. The thin vampire smelled like a wet sewer rat.

"Normally, you'd be my afternoon snack," Fang said. "But I've got better plans for you. You're going to be bait. Old Blood will come looking for you soon. And we'll be waiting for him."

Fang walked to the door of his room. "I got some business to take care of, Bait. Don't touch my stuff while I'm gone."

Fang slammed the stone door behind him, and Ivan's whole body went as limp as cooked spaghetti.

Focus, Ivan, he told himself. *There's got to be a*

way out of here.

Ivan began a careful search of the room. All of the garbage made it hard to find anything. But then something caught his eye.

A large poster for the band the Screaming Skulls had been stuck to the wall. But around the poster, Ivan could see deep crevices in the wall. He quickly pulled down the poster to reveal a door in the wall.

Ivan's heart beat quickly. He opened it.

Behind the door were two passageways leading to two different tunnels. Ivan knew he had to act fast. Which tunnel should he choose?

If Ivan goes through the tunnel on the left, go to page 18.

If Ivan goes through the tunnel on the right, go to page 91.

Continued from page 133

"Count Blood! It's sundown!"

Ivan opened the door to Count Blood's room—
the room Fang had taken over. The rock posters
and litter had been removed, and the room was
neat and clean.

Count Blood sat up in his stone coffin. "I can
still smell that fiend here," he said, sighing. "Vat
an odor!"

Ivan knew what the count meant. When Fang
had lived here, the place had smelled like mold, corn
chips, and something resembling rotten tomatoes.
He held up a mop and a bucket containing a bottle
of cleaning fluid. "I borrowed these from Nana," he
said. "We'll get this place back to normal."

Count Blood climbed out of his coffin and
stretched. "I have a busy night ahead of me, Ivan.
There is a group of verevolves terrorizing hamburger
restaurants. They must be stopped."

Ivan grinned. Count Blood was a real-life
superhero. And he was confiding in *him*, Ivan, a
regular kid. This was better than a comic book.

"Before I go, I have somethink to ask you, Ivan,"
Count Blood said, his voice serious.

Ivan nodded.

"My vork is very dangerous," the count began.

Ivan's heart sank. He knew what was coming.

The count was going to tell him he didn't want Ivan hanging around anymore.

"And you have shown a brave face in danger," the count continued. "I believe that you found the medallion for a reason. You see, I created the medallion in hopes of finding a suitable partner to vear it. Ivan, if you think I am vorthy, I vould like you to be my sidekick."

Ivan couldn't believe what he was hearing. "Me? A superhero? Like you? But I don't have any special powers."

"You have the medallion," Count Blood said. "And you are smart and brave. Those are the best qualities a superhero can have."

"Then I'll do it!" Ivan said. "I'll be your sidekick, Ivan Melchik."

"Of course, you vill need a super-hero name to protect your identity," said the count.

Ivan thought about all of the sidekicks in his comic books. He searched his mind. His name would have to be cool . . .

Then he remembered one of the last things Fang had said to him and smiled.

"How about Bat Boy?" he asked.

Count Blood nodded. "Very vell," he said. "Come, Bat Boy. Let us go fight some verevolves!"

THE END

Continued from page 65

There was something about Sasha that Ivan didn't like—or trust. He quickly thought of a way to get her off Count Blood's scent.

"Count Blood told me he was going to the abandoned mines in Bleaktown Hills," Ivan lied. "That's all I know."

Sasha studied Ivan's face and scowled. "You wouldn't lie to me, would you?" Her dark eyes seemed to stare right through Ivan's body.

"No," Ivan said, avoiding her glance.

"Fine," Sasha said, her voice cold. "I'll check out the mines. But if you're putting me on, I'll be back. That's a promise."

Then she took a business card from her jacket and handed it to Ivan.

"Call me if Blood shows up here," she said. Then she turned and walked down the stairs. Ivan felt his whole body relax.

Nana turned the corner and passed Sasha. She eyed her suspiciously, then ran up to Ivan.

"Who was that?" Nana asked.

Ivan thought quickly. "She was selling magazine subscriptions," he said. "I told her we didn't want any."

"Good," Nana said. "But you should not have opened the door, Ivan. I thought I taught you better than that." She shook her head and ushered him back inside.

Nana finished the soup soon after, and she and Ivan ate in silence. Ivan knew he didn't have much time before Sasha found out the truth—and he believed she would come back. He'd have to warn Count Blood right away.

"Nana, can I take a walk?" he said, pushing his empty soup bowl aside. "I need some fresh air."

Nana hesitated. "A young boy needs fresh air. You can help me clean the closets tomorrow."

"Thanks, Nana," Ivan said, relieved. He quickly washed his soup bowl in the sink. Then he ran out the back door.

Mount Hope Cemetery wasn't too far away. Tombstones, crypts, and statues rose up from the neatly landscaped green grass. Ivan walked through the iron gates, then stopped.

How was he going to find Count Blood? There must be hundreds of places he could be.

There must be a way to narrow it down, Ivan thought. *Where would I sleep if I were a vampire?*

His eyes traveled to the stone crypts that dotted the cemetery. Each one was the size of a small garden shed. They could easily fit one or more coffins. Count Blood must be in one of those. But which one?

Ivan knew that the oldest graves in the cemetery

were in the back, farthest from the gate. He'd start there. He couldn't imagine the count housed up in one of the newer, pearly marble crypts found in the front.

He hiked to the back of the cemetery. It seemed darker back there, and even a little chillier. There were more trees lining the paths, and their leafy branches let very little sunlight through.

Ivan started with the oldest-looking crypts. They were made of old, gray stone. Dark green moss and vines crept up the sides. Ivan walked up to one, and saw a name engraved above the door: HAMILTON.

The names could be a clue, Ivan realized. He searched his mind for Count Blood's original name. Blood was his vampire name, but he had another name. The name he had been born with . . .

VAN VALEN. The name popped into Ivan's mind. Excited, he ran from crypt to crypt, looking for the name.

And then Ivan found it. An old stone crypt with the name Van Valen engraved above the door. Ivan carefully pushed the door to the crypt aside.

He found himself in a small room with a low ceiling. A polished black coffin took up most of the space. Ivan closed the door behind him, plunging the crypt into darkness. Then he took a deep breath and knocked on the coffin lid.

"Count Blood?" he asked. "Count Blood, are you there?"

The coffin lid creaked open by itself, and Ivan saw Count Blood's pale face resting on a silk pillow. The vampire opened his eyes.

"Ivan, is that you?" he asked.

"It's still daylight," Ivan warned. "But I had to find you. A woman came looking for you. A vampire hunter. She said her name was Sasha."

Count Blood sat up in his coffin. He looked grave. "Sasha Varing. The daughter of Simon Varing, vampire hunter."

Ivan knew the name. Simon Waring had appeared in the comic book often—hunting for Count Blood.

"Sasha said you were evil," Ivan said. "But I didn't believe her. There was something really creepy about her."

Count Blood nodded. "Simon Varing alvays had an intense hatred for me. He refused to believe that a vampire could do good. He passed that belief onto his daughter. She vill hunt me until I am dust once again."

"I told her you went to the Bleaktown Mines," Ivan said. "But she's going to come back to my house when she finds out I'm lying. What should I tell her?"

Count Blood looked thoughtful. Then he

brightened. "You can tell her that you do not know vhere I am. But you know somethink better? You can lead her to Fang. She vants Fang almost as bad as she vants me."

"I don't know where Fang is," Ivan said.

"But I do," Count Blood said. "Vhile Sasha is busy vith Fang, I can figure out how to avoid her."

"But you're good, and Fang's evil," Ivan pointed out. "What if Fang hurts her?"

Count Blood shrugged. "She has chosen the life of a vampire hunter. The risk is hers."

Ivan wasn't sure what to do. He had just wanted to warn Count Blood about Sasha. He didn't want to get involved with any plan. What if something happened to Sasha? He didn't like her, but he didn't want her to get hurt, either.

If Ivan tells Sasha how to find Fang, go to page 77.

If Ivan refuses to go along with Count Blood's plan, go to page 66.

"I am not sure vat Fang vill do," Count Blood admitted. "It has been years since ve last fought and he defeated me."

"Then let's check out your old headquarters," Ivan said. "He won't be expecting us to go there. We can stay out of sight."

"I must admit I am curious," Count Blood said. "But are you sure you vant to accompany me, Ivan? Fang is very dangerous."

Ivan took a deep breath. This was the most exciting thing that had ever happened in his life. He didn't have any close friends, and he spent most of his time reading about other people's adventures in his comic books. Now it was his turn to have an adventure.

"I'm sure," Ivan replied.

Count Blood nodded. "I can see it vould be no use to discourage you. Very vell, then. Ve vill go. But first, let me tell you something about Fang.

"All vampires are different," Count Blood continued. "Ve have different strengths and veak-nesses. For example, I can turn into a bat, but that ability is very rare. Fang's strength is his power—he is physically much stronger than I. But he does have one veakness—a veakness I discovered just before he nearly destroyed me."

"What kind of veakness—I mean, weakness?" Ivan asked. He hadn't read anything about a weakness in the comic book.

"Most vampires cannot vithstand the touch of holy vater—vater blessed in a church," the count explained. "But Fang, he cannot touch any kind of vater at all. It is like poison to him."

"Weird," Ivan said. "It's like he's some kind of mutant vampire or something."

"As I said, all vampires have their strengths and veaknesses," Count Blood said. "Fang has managed to become very powerful despite his veakness. He has many followers. But I believe if I can destroy Fang, his followers vill scatter."

Before they left, Ivan found a plastic spray bottle under the sink and filled it with water. It couldn't hurt. He tied a piece of string around the neck and then attached the bottle to his belt loop. He stuffed more garlic into his back pocket, along with the cross he had made. When he was ready, Ivan and Count Blood headed out into the night.

This time, they went right to the Bleaktown Historical Society, a crumbling stone building just near Town Hall. Count Blood led Ivan behind the building, where a small plot of ancient gravestones sat, surrounded by a decrepit wood fence. The count walked to one of the tombstones. Its face, weathered over time, was smooth and blank.

The count pressed down on the top of the tombstone.

Immediately, the ground in front of the stone began to sink. Count Blood beckoned for Ivan to join him. Ivan jumped in front of the vampire and steadied himself as the grassy patch of ground sank into the earth like some kind of strange elevator.

They stopped moving. Ivan saw they were at the start of a long, dark tunnel illuminated by torches attached to the stone walls.

"This vay," Count Blood said. "I think I know vhere Fang might be."

Count Blood led Ivan through what seemed like a maze of tunnels, turning left, then right, then left again. Suddenly, he stopped and peeked around the next corner.

Ivan peeked, too. They had come to a room filled with coffins. Inside each coffin was a sleeping vampire. Ivan recognized the tattooed vampire from the day before.

Count Blood took a step back. "Such lazy vampires, Fang's crew," he whispered. "Alvays sleeping late."

Count Blood silently stepped into the room and glided past the coffins. Ivan nervously followed him, holding his breath. The count stopped in front of a blood red door and raised his hand.

A white light glowed from the count's hand. It hit the doorknob, and the door opened without a sound. Count Blood stepped inside, and Ivan followed.

They stepped into a round, stone room. Posters of heavy metal bands covered the gray walls. Clothes, CDs, and empty snack bags littered the floor. In the center of it all was a large, stone crypt.

Count Blood moved to the crypt and looked inside. A slow smile spread across his face.

"Ah, Fang," he said. "My revenge vill be sveet!"

"That's what you think, Blood!"

A vampire sat up in the crypt. He had a long, thin face, scraggly blond hair, and wore a red T-shirt emblazoned with a neon yellow skull. Ivan recognized him from the comic book—it was Fang!

Fang pointed his long, skinny fingers at Count Blood. Jagged red light, like tiny lightning bolts, sprang from his hands.

Count Blood raised his hands in defense. Glowing white light streamed from his fingers. Fang's blast dissolved harmlessly as soon as it hit the white light.

"You've been asleep too long, Blood, old boy," Fang said, jumping out of the crypt. "I've learned a few tricks since I last dusted you."

Fang jumped up in the air and hovered there for a second. Then he delivered a sharp kick to Count Blood's chest. The kick sent the older vampire reeling backward.

It all happened so fast that Ivan stood, frozen, for a second. Then he remembered the water bottle around his belt. He reached for his side.

Suddenly, he felt an arm around his throat. Ivan craned his neck to see the tattooed vampire behind him. He had Ivan pinned.

"I'll help you in a second, Fang," the vampire called out. "I'm gonna have a little snack first!"

The vampire lowered his face, his sharp fangs bared. Ivan thought quickly. He had one free arm. He could jab the vampire with his elbow and try to get away. Or he could reach for the garlic in his back pocket.

If Ivan jabs the vampire with his elbow, go to page 81.

If Ivan tries to grab the garlic, go to page 111.

The sound of footsteps came closer. Ivan had to do *something*. He decided to put on the medallion. He slipped the medal around his neck.

Suddenly, Ivan's skin began to tingle. Each and every muscle in his body cramped up at once. He moaned and sank to the floor.

Ivan's head began to pound, and a blinding light flashed in front of his eyes. He squeezed them shut.

"What's happening?" Ivan cried, but his voice ended in a strange squeaking sound.

Startled, Ivan opened his eyes.

Ivan had changed. Where his arms should be were two brown, leathery wings ending in claw-like hands. Ivan couldn't see his legs at all. On their own, his wings began to flap, and he fluttered up off the floor.

Then the truth hit Ivan.

"*Squeak!*" he cried.

He was trying to say, "I'm a bat!" But only a squeak came out.

Then Ivan heard a voice behind him.

"What do you know?" It was Fang. "Looks like boy wonder here has turned into a bat!"

Ivan found a crevice in the wall and huddled there, shaking with fear. Fang put his face close to Ivan's.

"Thanks for finding Blood's secret chamber for me," he said. "I've been wondering where he kept his other medallion. Guess I'll be taking that now."

Ivan looked down and realized the medallion still hung around his neck. Fang reached up to grab it.

A sudden wave of courage burst through Ivan. He flew out of the crevice and sailed past Fang's face.

"Get back here!" Fang screamed.

Ivan flew as fast as he could, trying to control his direction. He soared out of the chamber, back down the tunnel, and through the door into Fang's room. He flew past the tattooed vampire and Rose.

"Get that bat!" Fang yelled behind him.

Ivan flew down a dark tunnel, his tiny heart beating quickly in his body.

Then the tunnel forked.

Ivan hesitated, hovering in midair. When Rose had led him to Fang, he hadn't been paying attention. He wasn't sure which way would lead to the cemetery.

If Ivan takes the right fork, go to page 121.

If Ivan takes the left fork, go to page 130.

"It's still dark out," Ivan said nervously. "You should have time to find a safe place."

Count Blood nodded. "I did not mean to impose. Please tell me. Vhere are ve?"

"Maple Street," Ivan answered.

"That is not far from Mount Hope Cemetery," the vampire said. "There is a nice qviet crypt there I used to sleep in from time to time. I vill see if it is still available."

Count Blood walked to Ivan's window. Then he turned to Ivan and bowed politely.

"Thank you for bringing me back to life," he said. "I vill not trouble you any further."

The vampire opened the window. Then, in a flash, he transformed into a huge black bat! Ivan gasped. But the bat flew out of the window and into the night.

Ivan closed the window and sat down on his bed, dazed. What had just happened? Had it all been real? Maybe he was dreaming.

Then Ivan looked at the cut on his finger, which was still bright red. That was real enough.

Ivan took off his glasses and rubbed his eyes. He had to make sense of this. In the morning . . . he yawned sleepily and fell back on the mattress.

It seemed like only five minutes had passed

when Ivan woke up. Bright sunlight streamed through the window, and Nana leaned over the bed, her hand on his forehead.

"Ivan, are you all right?" she asked. "You are sleeping so late!"

Ivan glanced at the clock. It wasn't even 9 a.m. yet. But that was late for Nana. And his parents were already home and asleep by now.

"It's vacation, Nana," he said sleepily. "Can't I please go back to sleep?"

Nana clucked her tongue. "It is not good for a young boy to be so lazy. Get up and help me with the laundry."

Ivan moaned and climbed out of bed. He immediately looked at his finger.

The line of the cut was still visible. So last night *had* been real. He hoped Nana didn't have too many chores for him today. He wanted to do some research to find out more about what had happened with Count Blood. Maybe he could find something on the Internet.

But Ivan didn't get a chance all morning. Nana kept him busy folding laundry, dusting furniture, and sweeping floors. While Ivan worked, Nana made a big pot of soup for lunch.

She was stirring the pot when she suddenly frowned and put down her spoon.

"I am out of parsley," she said. "I must go to

the market. Be a good boy, Ivan, while I am gone."

"Sure, Nana," Ivan answered. He felt a sense of relief. He'd have at least a few minutes to go on the computer while she was gone.

Nana put on her sweater, grabbed a canvas tote bag, and left through the back door.

"Be good, Ivan!" she warned again.

Ivan sighed and then made a beeline for the family room. He was about to switch on the computer when he heard the front doorbell ring.

Ivan walked to the door and stood on his tiptoes to look out the small window. A striking-looking woman stood there. She had long, black hair. She wore a close-fitting leather jacket, jeans, and black boots. Ivan had never seen her before.

Ivan kept the chain on the door and opened it a crack.

"Can I help you?" he asked, as Nana had always taught him to do.

"I need to talk to you about Count Blood," the woman answered.

Ivan's heart pounded. Count Blood? Did she know about what had happened last night? Ivan cautiously opened the door and stepped out onto the front steps.

"What do you know about Count Blood?" Ivan asked.

"The question is, what do *you* know about him?" she replied. "Name's Sasha. I hunt vampires. And Count Blood is the worst. Last night I got a tip that Count Blood might be here. Do you know anything about it?"

"But Count Blood's a superhero," Ivan said defensively.

Sasha laughed. "You believe everything you read in comic books? That's all fiction. In real life, Blood is a dangerous criminal. I've got to stop him before he hurts innocent people. If you know where he is, you'd better tell me."

Ivan didn't like the threatening tone of her voice. But he wasn't sure what to do. If Sasha was right, it was his duty to help catch Count Blood. He was a vampire, after all.

But Count Blood *could* have hurt Ivan last night, and he didn't. In fact, he was downright polite. If he was so dangerous, why did he leave Ivan alone?

Ivan thought about his answer. He could tell Sasha the truth. Or he could give her a false lead—and go warn Count Blood himself.

If Ivan tells Sasha where Count Blood is, go to page 32.

If Ivan sends Sasha on a goose chase so he can warn Count Blood, go to page 50.

Continued from page 54

"Sorry," Ivan said. "If Sasha comes back, I'll try to stall her. That'll give you time to get away tonight. But that's all I'm willing to do."

"Sasha is very dangerous, Ivan," Count Blood said. "You vould be better off giving her Fang than nothing at all."

Ivan knew Count Blood was probably right. But he also had a secret weapon that Count Blood didn't know about—Nana.

"Don't worry," Ivan said. "If she comes around again, she won't get very far." Ivan held out his hand. "It was an honor meeting you, Count. Good luck with everything."

Count Blood shook Ivan's hand. The vampire's fingers felt cold in Ivan's palm.

"Be vell, Ivan," he said. "Thank you again for reviving me."

"It was an accident," Ivan said honestly. "But I'm glad I did it."

Count Blood's warning about Sasha haunted Ivan as he walked home. He wasn't looking forward to Sasha coming back. He'd feel better when he was home with Nana.

But when he got home, he found a note from his grandmother at the kitchen table.

Ivan—

Mildred invited me out for dinner at the Crab Shack and Bingo. I figure if you get a vacation, I should, too. There's goulash on the stove. Make sure your parents get up by five.

Love,

Nana

Ivan frowned and looked at the clock. At least it was almost time for his parents to get up.

Ivan read comic books until five o'clock. Then he woke up his parents. As long as Ivan could remember, his parents had both worked the night shift at the hospital. He saw them at dinnertime, and not much else.

The sun had set by the time the family sat down and ate Nana's goulash with bread and salad. Ivan always thought he looked like a mix of both of his parents: His father was short and round, with light hair, and his mother was tall and thin, but with dark hair and glasses. Ivan politely answered questions about his vacation—leaving out the part about Count Blood, of course.

His parents left for work at seven, leaving Ivan alone and wondering about Nana. He had settled down in front of the television when he heard the front door open.

That's odd, Ivan thought. *Nana always comes through the back.*

Then Sasha stormed into the living room, an angry look on her face. Ivan jumped off the couch, his heart racing.

"I didn't trust you, Ivan," Sasha said. "So I did a little research. Now I know why you lied to me."

Sasha reached into her jacket and pulled out a long, sharp wooden stake.

"You're a vampire, Ivan," she said. "You and your whole family. And I'm going to dust you all!"

Sasha was crazy—she had to be. Ivan knew there was no point arguing with her. He bolted off the couch.

If Ivan runs to the back door, go to page 97.

If Ivan runs to the front door, go to page 114.

Continued from page 25

"Maybe we could try finding Count Blood's coffin," Ivan suggested. "It sounds easier than doing the spell. And if we go there now, we'll have plenty of time before sunset."

Coburn looked at his watch. "I've got to paint mermaids in the ladies room at the Crab Shack today. I can meet you at the historical society at three. That'll still give us plenty of time."

Ivan thought over the plan as he rode the bus back to Bleaktown. Dave Coburn seemed to know what he was talking about. And the plan seemed simple enough. What could go wrong?

But a few hours later, as he stood under the shade of a willow tree next to the Bleaktown Historical Society, Ivan began to worry. Dave Coburn was more than an hour late.

Finally, Coburn showed up. Colorful paint now streaked his T-shirt.

"You're late," Ivan accused. "It's getting close to sunset. Maybe we should come back tomorrow."

"Who's the Count Blood expert here, me or you?" Coburn asked. "I know exactly where we're going. We'll be in and out in no time. Follow me."

Ivan obeyed, and Coburn walked to the back of the historical society building. A small graveyard sat there, surrounded by a rickety fence. Ancient tombstones rose up from the ground like crooked teeth.

Coburn's confidence had calmed Ivan a little. He felt even better when Coburn strolled up to one gravestone and pressed down on the top. Immediately, the tombstone began to sink into the earth—along with the rectangle of ground in front of it.

"Going down!" Coburn joked. Ivan ran to his side and braced himself as they sank deeper into the earth, like they were riding some kind of elevator.

"First floor, vampires," Coburn said as they stopped.

They had landed in an underground tunnel. Coburn stepped forward. "Follow me," he said.

The two walked in silence down the tunnel. Then the tunnel came to a T, and Coburn stopped.

"Left," he said, but his voice sounded unsure.

It soon became apparent they were in an underground maze. Coburn made turn after turn and Ivan felt nervous again.

"Are you sure you know where we're going?" he whispered.

"Of course," Coburn said. "I've been here hundreds of times."

They walked down a tunnel, and then Ivan

realized they were back where they started—at the first T.

"Maybe we should make a right this time," Ivan said.

"I knew that," Coburn said gruffly.

They made a right turn, and this time the tunnel led them to a stone door marked with a bat. Coburn smiled and pushed it open.

They stepped into a small chamber. In the center was a beautiful mahogany coffin. Silver candelabras stood in each corner, each one flickering with candlelight.

"Easy as pie," Coburn said. He stepped up to the coffin. "Blood won't wake up until sunset. We open the lid, slip on the medallion, and he's a good—"

The coffin lid swung open by itself. Count Blood sat up and grabbed Coburn around the neck.

"Nice to see you again, old friend," Count Blood said. "You are just in time for my breakvast."

"Kid, throw me the medallion!" Coburn yelled.

Ivan hesitated. Dave Coburn talked a lot, but he hadn't done anything right so far. Maybe it would be safer to run—and leave Coburn to Count Blood.

If Ivan runs, go to page 40.

If Ivan throws the medallion to Dave Coburn, go to page 84.

Continued from page 39

"Let's try, '*force of rock*,'" Ivan said quickly.
Coburn nodded. They began the spell again.
Depth of sea.
Force of rock.
Light of moon.
Power of sun.
May thy powers be undone."

Once again, they said the words three times—
but faster, this time, because Fang had begun to
circle the cemetery, sniffing around. He stopped in
front of their clump of bushes just as they finished
the last word.

Ivan held his breath. Had he remembered the
right words?

It didn't look that way. Fang spread apart the
bushes and glared at them. Up close, he smelled
like a combination of dirty socks and moldy cheese.

"Well, well," he said. "What do we have here?"

Fang motioned with his hand, and two of the
vampires in leather jackets ran up. One grabbed
Ivan, and the other grabbed Coburn.

"If I didn't know any better, I'd say this was
some kind of ambush," Fang said. Fang stopped in
front of Coburn and leaned in closer. "Dave, is that
you? You look old, man."

"Back off, creep!" Coburn sputtered.

"Man, mortality can be a bummer, can't it?" he asked. Then he stuck his face in Ivan's. "And who's this?"

"None of your business," Ivan said. He tried to sound as tough as Coburn, but it came out pretty weak.

"Fresh," Fang said. "But not much of a threat."

Fang turned his back to them and snapped his fingers.

"Take care of them," he said. "We'll show Blood he can't play games with us!"

Ivan felt two sharp fangs prick his neck. He tried to break away, but the vampire had him in a tight grip.

Then Count Blood emerged from his secret entrance. "Let them go, Fang!" he boomed.

"Well, well," Fang said. "I knew you'd show up. These friends of yours?"

"Let them go," the count repeated.

Fang stroked his beard. "Now this is interesting," he mused. "Looks like I've got the upper hand once again. With a snap of my fingers, your buddies are toast. You got that?"

Count Blood nodded.

"So don't try anything," Fang said. "Or I'll do it."

"Vat do you vant?" Count Blood asked.

"I want you gone. Out of my hair," Fang said. "Dusting you didn't work. So split. Scram. If I ever see you again, I'll take out my anger on your little friends."

"You have my vord," Count Blood said. "Let them go first."

Fang seemed satisfied. "I know your word is good. Unlike mine." He chuckled. Then he motioned to two vamps holding Ivan and Coburn.

"Count, no!" Coburn cried. "Don't do it. It's not worth it!"

Count Blood turned to them. "Thank you for helping me. I did not mean to put you in danger. Now run."

Ivan and Coburn hesitated.

"Go! Now!" Count Blood boomed.

Ivan and Coburn ran for the car. After they climbed in, Ivan looked behind him and saw Count Blood transforming into a bat.

"Look!" Ivan cried, pointing out the window. The large bat flew over the top of the historical society and into the distance.

"This stinks," Coburn muttered as he started the car.

Ivan felt terrible. He obviously hadn't remembered the words correctly. Ivan looked out the window and sighed.

"Sorry," he whispered. "I guess I failed you."

THE END

"All right! I'll try!" Ivan yelled.

He picked up the comic book and began to chant the spell backwards.

"Restored be away taken been has what let.
Sky and sea the of powers the by.
Done be undone been has what let.
Elements the of powers the by."

Ivan looked up from the comic book.

An army of skeletons had clawed their way out of the earth. He heard Coburn cry out behind him, and saw him fighting off three skeletons with his bare hands.

"Nice try, but not good enough!" Coburn yelled.

The salt. He'd have to try the salt. Ivan reached down to grab it . . .

A skeleton grabbed him by the ankle, and he fell facedown into the grass. Ivan kicked and screamed. Then he felt Coburn's hands on his shoulders, pulling him up.

"Let's go, kid," he said. "We'd better run."

Ivan didn't argue. Coburn pushed through skeleton after skeleton as they ran through the small cemetery.

Overhead, the sky suddenly grew dark. Lightning flashed across the sky, and thunder rumbled in the distance.

They ran to the car. Ivan risked a quick look back. The skeletons had collapsed into harmless piles of bones.

"Thank goodness," he said, turning back to the car.

Then he stopped.

Count Blood blocked their way. His eyes flashed with red light.

"So you tried to stop me," he said. "That vill be the last thing either of you do."

"*Noooooooo!*" Ivan screamed.

But a clap of thunder drowned out his cries.

THE END

Ivan decided that Count Blood was right. Sasha was a vampire hunter, after all. Why not give her a vampire to hunt? If she decided to go after Fang, she would be responsible for whatever happened. Besides, Ivan hadn't liked her very much, anyway.

"All right," Ivan said. "Let's send her after Fang. So you know where he is?"

Count Blood nodded. "Many years ago, there vas an amusement park outside Bleaktown. It vas destroyed by fire. Fang and his followers claimed the park for their own. I am sure they are still there."

"Do you think this will get Sasha off our backs?" Ivan asked.

"For a little vhile," Count Blood said. "That vill give me time to think of vhat to do next."

"All right, then," Ivan said. "I'll go home and call her. She gave me a card with her number on it."

"Good," said Count Blood. "I vould not like you to see her again, Ivan. She is a dangerous voman." Count Blood started to lie down in his coffin again, then hesitated. "I vill come see you after sundown, Ivan. To make sure you are all right."

The vampire settled back in his coffin, and Ivan closed the lid. Then he left the crypt, being careful to shut the door behind him.

Back home, Ivan found his grandmother busy pounding a mound of dough on the kitchen table. He quietly went to the living room and picked up the phone there. He took the card Sasha had given him and dialed the number.

"Hello?" Ivan recognized the vampire hunter's gruff voice.

"It's Ivan Melchik," he began nervously.

"Is Blood there?" she snapped. "I've been searching the hills, but there's no sign of him. If I found out you were lying to me—"

"I was lying to you, but it's not what you think," Ivan said, ready to launch into the story he had prepared on his walk back from the cemetery. "I don't know where Count Blood is. But you scared me. I had to tell you something."

"You haven't even seen how scary I can be!" Sasha said angrily.

"Let me finish," Ivan continued. "I've never met Count Blood. But I have met Fang. And I know where he is—him and his whole crew. I can tell you."

There was silence on the other end. Finally, Sasha spoke. "Fang, huh?" she said. "You'd better not be lying to me."

"Not this time," Ivan said, crossing his fingers. It wasn't exactly a lie. "Fang lives in the abandoned amusement park outside Bleaktown.

Go see for yourself."

"All right," Sasha said. "I'll check it out. But if you're messing around with me, you'll regret it!"

Ivan held the phone away from his ear as Sasha slammed down the phone on her end. Then he breathed a sigh of relief. Sasha had believed him. She'd find Fang, and either win or lose the fight. Either way, Ivan was out of it.

His nana stepped into the living room. "Ivan, Millie invited me out to dinner at the Crab Shack to celebrate her birthday. I figured since you're having a vacation, I might as well have one, too."

"Sure, Nana," Ivan said. "That's a good idea."

"There's goulash on the stove," she said, taking off her apron. "Don't forget to wake up your parents, Bubby, okay?"

"Okay." Mr. and Mrs. Melchik both worked the night shift at the hospital. They woke up at supper time and went to sleep before Ivan had his breakfast.

Ivan pulled out his Count Blood comic books and began to read them over again. This time, he focused on the stories about Simon Waring, Sasha's father. He was a tall, fierce-looking man who was determined to destroy Count Blood.

Ivan was engrossed in the books when Nana kissed him good-bye. He kept reading until he looked up and noticed the clock. It was almost time to wake up his parents. Ivan stood up and stretched lazily. Then he heard a knock on the door.

"Count Blood?" Ivan walked to the door and opened it. It was just sunset now. Could the count have traveled here so quickly?

Sasha stood in front of the door. Without warning, she grabbed Ivan and pulled his hands behind his back. Ivan struggled as Sasha tied a rope tightly around his wrists. Then she pushed him out the door.

"I got to thinking," Sasha said. "I double-checked with my sources. They said you definitely had contact with Count Blood, not Fang. Maybe you're lying about Fang; maybe you're not. But Blood's the one I want. And I think you're in league with him."

"What do you want me for?" Ivan asked as she pushed him down the walk. "I'm not a vampire. I'm just a kid!"

Sasha grinned. "Easy, Ivan. You're bait!"

Go to page 106.

Continued from page 59

Ivan had to make his decision in a millisecond, and he reacted mostly on instinct. He jabbed the vampire with his elbow, which was the quickest action he could take.

The jab didn't hurt the tattooed vampire at all; in fact, it made him laugh.

"Ooh, my snack thinks he's tough," joked the vampire. "I hope I don't get indigestion."

Ivan didn't give up. He stomped on the vampire's bare foot.

"Ow!" the vampire cried. Startled, he let go of his grip on Ivan.

Ivan pulled the spray bottle off his belt and pointed it at Fang. The skinny vampire had cornered Count Blood, and his hands were raised for another attack.

"Don't move!" he told the tattooed vampire. "Or your boss gets a bath!"

Fang turned away from Count Blood. "No!" he cried.

The other vampires, awake now, had gathered at the door to Fang's room. They backed away, looks of horror on their faces.

"Easy now, kid," said the tattooed vampire. "Put down that thing and we'll let you go."

Ivan took a deep breath. Here was his chance

to be a hero. One squirt and Fang would be gone, like that.

But before Ivan could pull the trigger, Fang lunged at him, knocking him on his back. The water bottle rolled out of his hands. A foul odor came off the vampire as he loomed over Ivan.

"I thought Blood would have better backup than this," Fang sneered. "Too bad for you, kid. You lose." Fang lowered his face to Ivan's neck.

"No, Fang. You lose."

Ivan saw Count Blood standing behind Fang. White light shot from his fingers and zapped Fang in the back.

Fang's fangs grazed Ivan's neck. Then he stopped, and a look of shock crossed his face.

"No way," he said. Then he exploded into countless grains of dust.

Ivan rose to his feet, brushing dust off his jeans. Count Blood faced Fang's henchmen now, his hands still raised in front of him.

"You vill go now," Count Blood demanded calmly. "You vill go and never return here."

Fang's men didn't argue. They scrambled out of the hideout like rats leaving a sinking ship.

Ivan looked at the pile of dust on the floor.

"Couldn't he come back, like you did?" Ivan asked.

Count Blood gave a small smile. "Not if ve

clean him up first."

The vampire picked up the water bottle and began to spray at the dust until it had completely dissolved.

"Good idea," Ivan said, grinning. "That guy really needed a bath!"

Go to page 95.

Continued from page 71

Ivan couldn't just leave Coburn there. He threw the medallion, and Coburn caught it with one hand. Then he jabbed Count Blood in the stomach with his elbow.

Count Blood gasped and Coburn pushed out of his grip. He turned around and gave Count Blood's coffin a push. The coffin, with Count Blood still inside, toppled off the stone pedestal it rested on.

Count Blood seemed to fly out of the coffin. He landed gracefully on his feet as the coffin clattered to the chamber floor.

"How dare you challenge me?" he asked Coburn.

Coburn crouched down in a fighting stance. "Bring it on, Count. Bring it on!"

Ivan watched, fascinated, as the vampire and the comic-book artist began to battle. Count Blood lunged at Coburn, who dropped to the ground and somersaulted out of the way. Then Coburn kicked out, slamming Count Blood in the knees.

The blow would have brought down a normal man, but Count Blood was a vampire with super-powers. He stumbled backward, then charged at Coburn. With one hand, he picked up the artist by the front of his T-shirt and lifted him two feet off the ground.

"You are foolish, Coburn," Count Blood said. "Alvays rushing into thinks vithout thinking."

"That might be what it looks like," Coburn replied. "But I can be surprising sometimes."

Coburn quickly held up the medallion. Since he was right above Count Blood's head, he easily slipped the medallion around his neck.

"So, Count," Coburn said. "Still want to fight?"

A surprised look crossed Count Blood's face. "I am so sorry, my friend," he said, setting Coburn back on the floor. "Vat has happened?"

"That big vampire tore off your medallion," Ivan said. "You turned evil."

Count Blood looked down at the medallion and patted it with his hand. "I remember," he said. "And now ve must flee. I told Fang's crew that I vould join their evil army. Fang vill be coming for me here tonight."

"Fleeing sounds good," Ivan agreed. He had enough scary vampire fights for one night.

They left the underground tunnels and emerged into the night air. Stars glittered in the deep purple sky overhead.

"We can take my car," Coburn said. "Let's go back to my place. We have a lot to talk about."

Ivan started the story as they drove, telling

Count Blood how he had tracked down Coburn.

"Very smart, Ivan," said Count Blood. "David knows my vays better than any other human."

Soon Dave pulled into his driveway. He handed Ivan a key.

"I'll be right back," he said. "You guys make yourselves at home."

Ivan entered Dave's dark house, feeling just a little bit nervous. Count Blood had been evil just a little while ago. Could he really trust him?

"I vill not harm you," Count Blood said, as if he had read Ivan's thoughts. "The medallion alvays vorks. If I have it on, of course."

"Sure," Ivan said. He turned on a lamp.

Ivan and the count stared at each other in silence until Dave came in, carrying a brown paper bag.

"One more second," he told them. He disappeared into the kitchen, and came back with a glass filled with red liquid.

"Pig's blood," he said proudly. "From the all-night butcher shop in Bleaktown. I figured you might be hungry."

"Thank you," said Count Blood. He took the glass from Coburn and took a sip. Then he smiled. "Qvite delicious!"

"I have to say, I've missed you, Count," Coburn said. "It hit me hard when Fang dusted you."

"It vas a terrible battle," Count Blood said. "Fang tricked me, you know. I vould very much like to see his reign of terror end."

"That stinks. You always fought fair," Ivan said. "Remember issue eighty-five? Dr. Mystic wanted to help you. He tried that spell to weaken Fang's powers. But you stopped him because you didn't want to have an advantage over Fang."

Count Blood sighed. "Foolish pride, perhaps. Now I vould do anything to defeat Fang. If only Dr. Mystic had not been trapped in the Tower of Ice. He vould still help us, I know."

A thought occurred to Ivan. "Maybe we don't need Dr. Mystic," he said. "We could do the spell ourselves, couldn't we? Dave wanted to use one of Dr. Mystic's spells to get rid of your evil, but we decided to go to your coffin instead. Why couldn't we do a spell now?"

Coburn's eyes shone. "That's not a bad idea," he agreed. "I remember the incantation: *Depth of sea. Strength of rock. Light of moon. Power of sun. May thy powers be undone.*"

"That might be it," Ivan said. It didn't sound exactly right to him.

"Dr. Mystic said it three times," Coburn remembered. "It's perfect. We go back to your hideout, Count. You said Fang was showing up there, right? When he shows, Ivan and I will do the spell. Then you can take down Fang—just like you should have all those years ago."

"We should look in issue eighty-five," Ivan suggested, "just to make sure the spell is right."

"I know it's right!" said Coburn. "Besides, I don't have any issues of *Count Blood* anymore. I sold them all when the lobster painting business got slow."

"I can go home right now and get mine," Ivan volunteered.

"Fang could get to the count's headquarters by that time," Coburn pointed out. "I know what I'm talking about. Let's just do it!"

Ivan frowned. If Coburn's memory was wrong, the plan would fail miserably. Could he trust the boastful comic-book artist?

If Ivan insists on getting the comic book, go to page 138.

If they decide to trust Coburn's memory, go to page 36.

Continued from page 19

Ivan decided putting on the medallion was too risky. His mind raced as he tried to think of another plan. But there was no time.

Fang ran into the chamber, an annoyed look on his face. But the expression disappeared as he gazed around the chamber.

"Hey, I never knew this was here," he said. He walked to the pedestal and scooped up the medallion. "This could be useful. Cool."

Then his eyes narrowed again as he looked at Ivan. "You escaping—not cool. But that's all right. I'll let you stay here until Blood shows up. Then—well, you won't be so safe anymore. So enjoy it while you can."

Ivan shivered. He didn't like the sound of that.

Fang walked back outside and looked at the wall. "These things usually work by pressing on a secret panel, right?" Ivan didn't say anything. Fang began pressing on stones until he hit the right one. The door began to slide shut, and the vampire grinned.

"See you later," he said. "I'll take care of you after I take care of Blood."

Ivan breathed a sigh of relief after Fang left. At least the vampire hadn't hurt him. He ran to the wall and began pounding on the stones. There had to be a way to open the door from the inside, right?

Apparently not, Ivan learned, after he had pounded on every stone in the chamber. He sank to the floor, dismayed.

And then he heard shouts outside the chamber. He heard Fang's voice, and the distinctive voice of Count Blood. But he couldn't make out what they were saying.

Ivan pressed his ear to the door, his heart pounding with excitement. Count Blood would defeat Fang. Then he'd find Ivan. He had to!

But the next sound he heard was a loud cry from Count Blood. There was silence, and then the noisy cheers of Fang and his crew.

Ivan's heart sank. Count Blood had been defeated. He knew it in his gut. And Fang would be coming for him next.

"I should have put on that medallion when I had the chance!" Ivan moaned.

THE END

Continued from page 47

Ivan decided to go down the tunnel on the right. He plunged inside, pushing the heavy door shut behind him.

The tunnel was pitch black, and Ivan had no idea how far it continued. He kept his right hand on one of the walls and ran down the tunnel as fast as he could.

Once again, Ivan found himself making turn after turn, as though he were some kind of rat caught in a maze. He finally stopped to catch his breath.

The tunnel was absolutely quiet. *At least Fang hasn't figured out I've escaped yet,* Ivan thought. *That should give me time to figure out how to leave this place.*

Ivan kept going, slower now. The air seemed to get colder with each step, and he shivered.

Then the ground opened up beneath his feet, and Ivan felt himself plummet into nothingness.

With a thud, he landed on cold, hard earth. He slowly rose to his feet and took inventory of his body parts. Everything seemed to be working. Somehow, his glasses had managed to stay on his face.

But where was he? Ivan couldn't see a thing in the dark. He began to feel the wall around him, taking slow steps.

He realized he was traveling in a circle. He had fallen into some kind of pit. Maybe he could climb out.

Ivan jumped up as high as he could, but he couldn't feel the top of the pit. He jumped again and again. It was no use.

Ivan sat down and tried to calm his mind. Something crawled across his ankle, and he cried out.

Calm down, Ivan, he told himself. Things weren't hopeless.

Count Blood could find him and rescue him. He was a superior supernatural being, after all.

Fang could find him and take him back to use as bait for Count Blood. That would be better than being trapped in a pit.

"Someone will find me," Ivan said.

He couldn't stay trapped in the pit forever. Could he?

THE END

Continued from page 35

Ivan took a *Count Blood* comic book out of his backpack and removed the paper bag protecting it. Then he carefully scooped up the dust in the coffin and put it in the plastic bag. He made sure he got every last grain.

Ivan carefully stored the bag in his backpack and left the cemetery. He walked to the downtown area and turned down Wary Lane.

Sebastian Cream's Junk Shop was there, just as it had been yesterday, when this had all started. Ivan stepped through the door and found Mr. Cream sitting on a stool behind the counter. He nodded when he saw Ivan.

"Back again, I see," he said. "Have you found the vial to be interesting?"

"I was kind of hoping you had another one," Ivan said.

Mr. Cream frowned. "Oh, dear," he said. "You didn't have an accident with the vial you bought, did you? Count Blood would be very upset."

Mr. Cream's comment startled Ivan. "What do you know about Count Blood?"

The shopkeeper stared at Ivan through his glasses. "About as much as you do, young man. One thing I do know is that the vial was one of a kind. Specially made to revive the ashes of a vampire."

Ivan was full of questions, but something told him that he wouldn't get much information from the strange little man. "You mean there's nothing else like it? Are you sure?"

Mr. Cream nodded. "If such an item existed, I would have heard of it."

Ivan frowned and patted his backpack. "If you ever get another one, could you please let me know? My name's—"

"Ivan Melchik," Mr. Cream said. "I certainly will do that, Ivan."

A creepy chill came over Ivan's body. He said good-bye and quickly left the store.

"Sorry, Count Blood," Ivan said out loud as he headed back home. "I'll try to find some way to bring you back again. I promise!"

THE END

Continued from page 83

"How's it going, Count?" Ivan asked.

Count Blood sat up in his crypt as Ivan entered, carrying a large envelope under his arm. The count's room had been stripped clean of the posters and trash that had littered it when Fang lived there. In its place was a sleek metal desk topped with a computer.

"I slept vell," Count Blood said. "And how are things going vith the comic book?"

Ivan beamed and opened the envelope. He pulled out several boards covered with black-and-white drawings.

"Wonder Comics sent us a copy of the first sketches to look over," Ivan said, spreading the boards out on the desk. "I knew you'd want to see them right away."

It was two months after the battle with Fang, and Count Blood was back in business as a super-hero, battling evil creatures of the night. Ivan had the idea to let the comic-book company know about it, and they had agreed to put out the *Count Blood* comic books again. They had even agreed to let Ivan write it!

Ivan and Count Blood bent over the boards. The drawings told the whole story, starting with Ivan cutting his finger and bringing Count Blood back to life. The last panel showed Count Blood turning into a bat and flying off into the night, ready to fight evil.

"Ivan, these are vonderful," Count Blood said. "I must thank you. Vithout you, I vould not be here today."

Ivan felt prouder than he ever had in his whole life. Not only had he helped Count Blood, but he was an honest-to-goodness comic-book writer, too! He thought back to that first day of school vacation, when he had wandered into Sebastian Cream's Junk Shop looking for comic books.

"None of this would have happened if I hadn't gone into that weird junk shop," Ivan remarked. "I'm sure glad I did!"

THE END

Ivan ran into the kitchen and threw open the back door. Before he could take a step outside, Sasha reached out and grabbed the back of his shirt.

"Soon there'll be one less monster in the world," she growled.

"Help!" Ivan screamed.

Then a dark figure swept through Ivan's back-yard.

"Count Blood!" Ivan cried.

Sasha let go of Ivan and stepped out into the yard. Ivan ran to Count Blood's side.

"Count Blood." She spat out his name. "So you've come to challenge me, have you?"

"No," the vampire replied coolly. "I have come to help my friend."

"Of course," Sasha sneered. "You monsters always stick together."

"Ivan is no monster," Count Blood said. "You should know better, Sasha."

Sasha frowned. "He's a Melchik. Even you must know that the Melchik clan stems from a line of blood-suckers."

Count Blood shook his head. "You are like your father in some vays, Sasha, but not others. The vampire line of the Melchiks vas destroyed in

1859 by your great-grandfather. The remaining Melchiks are all human."

Then Ivan remembered something. "When you came to see me, I stood in the sunlight," he said. "How could I do that if I was a vampire?"

A look of recognition flickered on Sasha's face. Then she frowned again. "No matter," she said. "I've got what I came here for in the first place. You."

Sasha whipped out a crossbow and a sharpened wooden spike from inside her jacket. In a flash, she sent the spike flying toward Count Blood.

The count jumped in the air and seemed to hover there for a few seconds. Then he silently landed on his feet.

Count Blood raised his hands in front of his face. Bolts of white light shot from his fingertips toward Sasha.

Sasha just grinned. "Your old tricks don't work anymore," she said, whipping a silver rod out from her jacket. A round crystal topped the rod. She thrust the rod in front of her face, and the crystal absorbed the lightning bolts, rendering them harmless.

Count Blood sped up his attack, shooting bolt after bolt at Sasha, but the crystal absorbed them all.

When the attack subsided, Sasha put down the rod and picked up the crossbow again, ready to shoot another wooden spike at the count.

Count Blood zapped the crossbow with a bolt, hoping to destroy it. Instead, the sharp spike let loose—and headed right for Ivan.

The vampire sprang into action. He jumped in front of Ivan, knocking him to the ground.

Ivan heard a scream. When he got back on his feet, Count Blood was gone.

In his place was a steaming pile of dust.

"Nooooo!" Ivan cried. Count Blood had been dusted trying to save him. It wasn't fair!

Then a thought crossed his mind. Count Blood had been turned to dust. Ivan had revived him once before. Maybe he could do it again.

But Sasha dashed his hopes. She walked up to the pile of dust. Then she took a glass tube out of her jacket and uncorked it. She poured a foul-smelling yellow liquid on the dust, which evaporated instantly.

"Good riddance," she said.

"You're wrong!" Ivan said angrily. "Count Blood was good. You saw what he did. He saved my life!"

Sasha shrugged. "Not my problem," she said. She studied Ivan. "I guess you're not a vampire after all. Still, you should be careful of the company you keep, Ivan Melchik. I don't like vampires. And I don't like humans who make friends with vampires, either."

Then Sasha walked off into the dark night.

Ivan stared at the ground where Count Blood had been, and a tear filled his eye. His slowly walked back into the house and sat at the kitchen table, his head in his hands.

Nana came through the back door a few minutes later. She carried a white paper bag with a picture of a crab on it.

"Are you hungry, Ivan?" she asked cheerfully. "I brought back leftovers."

Then she saw Ivan's sad face. "Bubby, what's wrong? You're sitting here all alone in the dark."

"Nothing, Nana," Ivan muttered.

Nana patted his head. "Why don't you go read one of your comic books? That might cheer you up."

"Don't feel like it," Ivan said. He'd only be reminded of Count Blood. If he had only listened to the vampire, none of this would have happened.

Then an idea popped into his mind.

Count Blood might be gone. But Ivan could share his story with others. He would write his *own* comic book. That way, Count Blood's memory would live on.

Ivan pushed away from the table. "Good night, Nana," he said. "I've got some work to do!"

THE END

Continued from page 129

Ivan knew he needed to do something—fast. And scattering the salt was the fastest solution—if it worked. He reached down and picked up the bowl of salt.

"Get back! Get back!" Ivan yelled. He ran around the grass, sprinkling salt everywhere he could.

Almost immediately, the earth stopped rumbling. The skeletal hands sank back into the ground. Green grass started to grow where the earth had been torn up.

Coburn walked up to Ivan and shook his hand. "Nice work, kid," he said.

"Thanks," Ivan said. "But we still haven't turned Count Blood good again."

Coburn looked thoughtful. "You know, I'm pretty sure the problem was the parsnip. Maybe we should get a ginger root and try that. What's the worst that could happen?"

Ivan stared at him. "You're kidding, right?"

Coburn shrugged. "You handled those skeletons pretty well. I'm sure if something goes wrong again, you can fix it."

Ivan suddenly felt proud. And even though he was still shaking from fright, defeating the skeletons made him feel confident.

"All right," he said. "I won't give up. Count Blood wouldn't."

They drove to a nearby market and got a gnarled piece of ginger root. Ivan agreed it looked much more like the picture than the parsnip did. He set up the blanket, water, and salt again, and set the ginger in the right place. Coburn took the parsnip and chucked it into the woods behind the society.

"Just in case," Coburn said.

Ivan sat cross-legged on the blanket and began to chant again.

"By the powers of the elements.
Let what has been undone be done.
By the powers of the sea and sky.
Let what has been taken away be restored."

Ivan looked around. So far, nothing had happened.

"Keep going, kid," Coburn called out. "I got a good feeling this time."

Ivan kept repeating the chant over and over. He put down the comic book and closed his eyes. Soon he felt the words coursing through his body, as though they had become part of him.

Then he heard Coburn's voice in his ear. "Kid, look!"

Ivan opened his eyes. A blue ball of light hovered in front of him. Ivan stared at it, mesmerized.

"Wow," he breathed.

Ivan watched as the ball floated around the cemetery. It stopped in front of one tombstone. Then it sank into the grass.

"Do you think it's working?" Ivan asked.

Coburn looked up at the sky. The sun was slowly sinking over the horizon.

"We won't have long to wait," he said.

Coburn sat on the blanket next to Ivan. They sat in silence until darkness settled over the cemetery.

Suddenly, a tall figure began to rise up from the ground.

"Count Blood!" Ivan cried. He almost got up and ran. What if Count Blood was still evil?

But the vampire looked different. Blue light bathed his whole body. He walked up to the blanket, smiling.

"Ivan, it is so good to see you," he said. "I am so sorry I tried to hurt you yesterday."

"That's okay," Ivan replied.

Then Count Blood turned to Coburn. "And you, old friend. It is good to see you."

"Thanks, Count," Coburn said. He turned to Ivan. "Better give him back his medallion before the spell wears off."

Ivan took the medallion from his pocket and handed it to Count Blood. The vampire put it around his neck.

"I cannot thank you enough. Both of you," Count Blood said.

"So what now?" Ivan asked. "Are you going to go after Fang?"

Count Blood's face darkened. "Yes. But not right now. I learned much last night. Fang has amassed a huge army of vampires. It vill take much planning to defeat him. That is, if you vill help me."

"Of course," Ivan said.

"Why not?" Coburn said. "Think we can talk about it over your nana's goulash?"

Ivan smiled. Days ago, he had a normal, boring life. The only excitement he got was from reading comic books.

And now his life was better than any comic book he had ever read.

"Let's go," Ivan said.

THE END

Continued from page 80

Sasha shoved Ivan into a small, black car and drove in silence until they reached a small house at the end of a dead-end street. She held tightly onto Ivan's bound hands and led him into the house through the back door.

They entered a small, neat kitchen with gleaming silver and black appliances, a metal table, one metal stool, and not much else. Sasha pushed him through into what would, in a normal house, have been the living room. But this room looked like an arsenal.

A vampire-hunting arsenal, that is. Racks of wooden stacks lined one wall. Another wall held bunches and bunches of dried garlic. A glass case held strange-looking weapons that Ivan couldn't recognize.

Sasha led Ivan to a black leather couch.

"Sit down," she said. "We won't have to wait long. After I take care of Blood, I'll let you go. I don't hurt humans."

"What makes you so sure the count will find us?" Ivan asked.

"If you and the count are in league, he'll come looking for you," she said. "I left a message for him at your house."

"Doesn't that prove he's a good vampire?" Ivan

pointed out. "If he were evil, why would he bother to come and save me?"

"He's probably afraid you'll give up his secrets to me," Sasha said. "Vampires aren't good, Ivan. They can't be."

Sasha walked to the glass case and took out a framed black-and-white photograph. She brought it over to Ivan.

"My father, Simon Waring, and I came from a long line of vampire hunters," she said. "Do you know why we hunt vampires?"

Ivan shook his head.

"The first Waring to hunt vampires lost his whole family to a vampire army," Sasha said, her face growing dark. "He vowed to devote his life to destroying those monsters of the night. And every generation, a member of the Waring family continues that promise."

"I get it," Ivan said. "But just because some vampires are bad doesn't mean that all of them are."

"They're all monsters," Sasha replied. "That is what my father taught me, and nobody fought more vampires than Simon Waring. I owe it to my dad to take out Count Blood. The count was his biggest rival."

Ivan knew there was no use reasoning with Sasha. He just hoped Count Blood could survive whatever attack she had in store for him.

Sasha returned the picture to the case and stood by the door, looking through the glass window.

Suddenly, something crashed through the window, sending glass shattering everywhere. Ivan jumped up, and Sasha immediately pulled a crossbow and wooden stake out of her jacket. A black bat flew around the room, its wings flapping wildly.

Then, before their eyes, the bat transformed into Count Blood. He stood in front of Ivan protectively.

"Let Ivan go now," Count Blood said. "He has nothink to do vith this."

"I'll let him go when I'm through with you, Count," she said, leveling the crossbow at him.

At that moment, the glass cabinet began to rattle wildly. Sasha's gaze left Count Blood. Ivan and the count turned toward the cabinet, too.

The photo of Simon Waring floated out of the cabinet. Then a ghostly image of Waring floated off the photo and hovered in front of Sasha.

"Dad?" Sasha asked, her eyes filled with tears.

"I was wrong, Sasha," Simon Waring said in a raspy voice. "The Warings have done important work. But not all vampires deserve to be destroyed. Count Blood is a hero, a protector of the innocent. I know this now. You must, too."

Sasha turned to the count, her eyes blazing. "It's a trick!"

"You must believe me, daughter," Simon said. He reached out with a ghostly hand and stroked her face. "Do what is right."

Then the ghostly image disappeared, and the picture frame dropped to the floor and crashed.

Sasha lowered the crossbow. Tears ran down her face.

"That was him," she whispered. "I know it."

Count Blood walked over and lightly touched Sasha's arm. "I vill not hurt you, Sasha," he said. "I do not hurt humans."

"It's true!" Ivan cried. "You've got to believe us now!"

"I do," Sasha said, collapsing into a chair. "I just wish I had more time with Dad. I mean, what do I do now? I'm a vampire hunter."

"You can still hunt vampires," Count Blood said. "There are many evil vampires out there. Fang, for example."

"Yeah," Ivan said. "I was telling the truth about where he is."

Sasha stood up, and a fire burned in her eyes once again. "Then let's get him. You and me, Count."

Count Blood nodded. "I vould like to see Fang

taken care of."

"We can go tonight," Sasha said. She ran to the wall and began pulling off weapons.

"Can I go?" Ivan asked. Things were getting exciting. It was a lot more fun to be hanging out with vampires and vampire hunters than to just be reading about them in comic books.

"It vould be very dangerous," Count Blood said.

"We'll take you home, Ivan," Sasha said. "Hunting vampires is not for kids."

So Sasha, Count Blood, and Ivan piled into Sasha's car. They left Ivan on his doorstep.

Ivan watched the car drive away. He started to go upstairs and then stopped.

He knew where they were going. Maybe—just maybe—he would go to the amusement park himself and watch the action up close. Why not?

If Ivan stays home, go to page 119.

If Ivan goes to the amusement park, go to page 134.

Continued from page 59

Ivan had no time to think. He tried to reach for the garlic in his back pocket—but the tattooed vampire grabbed his hand and gripped it tightly.

"No funny moves, snack!" he growled.

The next thing Ivan felt was a sharp pain as the vampire's fangs poked into his neck. He closed his eyes. Count Blood was right. He never should have come here!

But the fangs never sank in, and Ivan felt the vampire loosen his grasp. He opened his eyes to see Count Blood hovering over the tattooed vampire. White light glowed from Count Blood's fingertips. The light zapped the vampire, who immediately turned into a pile of dust on the floor.

"Thanks," Ivan said.

Count Blood had no time to reply. The other vampires, roused from their sleep, charged into the room. They attacked Count Blood at once.

Terrified, Ivan crawled into a corner and watched the battle. Count Blood zapped the vampires one by one. Some of them turned to dust; others turned and ran.

Then Ivan saw a skinny figure run up behind Count Blood. Fang! Ivan had forgotten all about him.

"Count, look out!" Ivan yelled.

But he was too late. Fang attacked Count Blood from behind, shooting red blasts from his hands. The jagged red light enveloped Count Blood and lifted him up off the floor.

"Nice try, Blood," Fang said. "But it looks like I've got you again."

"Go ahead," said Count Blood. "Dust me. At least I vill die an honorable death."

"I don't think so," Fang said. "It might be more fun to *dis*honor you. You know the code, Blood. I beat you twice. Now you've got to scram."

A dark look crossed Count Blood's face, but he nodded. "I vill honor the code," he said. Then he motioned toward Ivan. "But you must let my friend go."

Fang shrugged. "Why not? He's useless."

Fang lowered his hands, and the circle of red light disappeared. Count Blood turned and walked out without saying a word. Ivan quickly followed him.

The two emerged back in the graveyard behind the historical society.

Ivan spoke first. "What's this about a code?"

"Fang has beaten me tvice," Count Blood said. "He has the right to banish me. I must go live out my days in exile. I cannot challenge Fang again."

"That's not fair!" Ivan cried.

"It is the code," Count Blood said. "Thank you for your help, Ivan. But now I must go."

Count Blood transformed into a bat. Ivan watched as he soared away into the night sky.

Ivan felt terrible.

"I can't believe this happened," he muttered. "I feel like it's all my fault."

THE END

Continued from page 68

Ivan didn't know where to go; he just knew he had to get away. He ran past Sasha toward the nearest exit—the front door. He yanked open the door, but before he could step out Sasha grabbed the back of Ivan's shirt and pulled him toward her.

"Help!" he screamed.

Then he saw his mom and dad walking up the front steps. He nearly cried with relief.

"She's crazy!" Ivan yelled. "She thinks we're vampires."

"Don't take another step," Sasha said behind him. "Or I'll dust the boy. I mean it."

"I don't think so," Ivan's dad said.

Then his eyes turned the color of blood.

"You're messing with the wrong family," said Ivan's mom. A low growl rose from her throat, revealing two sharp fangs.

Ivan gasped. What was going on?

Mr. and Mrs. Melchik both raised their arms in front of them. Suddenly, green light shot from their fingertips. The light zapped Sasha, and she let go of her grip on Ivan.

Ivan ran to his parents. He turned and faced Sasha, who was enveloped in a sizzling bubble of green light.

"We could destroy you, but we will not," said Mrs. Melchik in an even voice. "We're not like you or your father, Sasha."

"No, you're not!" Sasha spat out. "You're monsters!"

Mr. and Mrs. Melchik exchanged glances. They nodded to each other. Then they both clapped their hands at the same time.

The green light exploded, and Sasha collapsed to the floor, her eyes closed.

Ivan's head was spinning. He took a step back from his parents. "Is she—"

"Unconscious," said Mr. Melchik. "For a few hours. We don't have much time."

"What's going on?" Ivan asked.

Just then, Nana came running up the steps.

"Oh, dear," she said. "I'm sorry I didn't get here sooner. Is Ivan all right?"

Mrs. Melchik nodded. "He is. But we need to have a talk with him."

Ivan followed his family into the kitchen. They all sat at the round kitchen table except for Nana, who fussed around them, putting on a kettle for tea and getting out mugs.

"I guess it's time you knew, Ivan," Mr. Melchik said. "That woman out there was right. Your mom and I are vampires."

Ivan felt like he was in some kind of dream.

He had seen his father's blood red eyes and his mother's fangs. He had watched what they did to Sasha. And as long as he could remember, they had only been out at night, never during the daylight. It could be true.

"But . . . how?" Ivan asked.

"We were born that way," his mother replied. Behind her thick glasses, her dark eyes were full of concern. "But we are not evil, Ivan. We don't hurt anyone."

"Some vampires do hurt people," said Mr. Melchik. "But not all of us. Even so, some humans—like Sasha—think all vampires should be exterminated, no matter what."

Ivan let the information sink in. Count Blood had said the same thing about Sasha, so that made sense. As far as his parents being born vampires . . . that left him with new questions— some easier than others.

"Is Nana a vampire?" Ivan asked.

"No," Nana replied, sitting down at the table. "Sometimes it skips a generation. That's why I'm able to take care of you while your parents are sleeping."

"So that's why I'm not a vampire, right?" Ivan said hopefully. "It skipped a generation?"

His parents exchanged glances again. Mr. Melchik answered.

"We do not know yet," Mr. Melchik said. "The change does not occur until a vampire turns thirteen. You probably are a vampire, Ivan, but we won't know for sure until your thirteenth birthday."

Me . . . a vampire? Ivan couldn't believe it. How would he go to school? What would he tell his friends? Would he ever be able to go to the beach again?

Then he realized that he didn't really like school, or the beach, and he didn't really have any friends. Maybe being a vampire wouldn't be so bad.

But Ivan didn't have time to worry about it. His mother sprang up from the table.

"We have to hurry," she said. "Ivan, go to your room and pack up as many things as you can. We've got to get out of here before Sasha wakes up."

"Now?" Ivan asked.

"She knows where we live," Mr. Melchik said. "We will never be safe here again."

Ivan ran up the stairs, his heart pounding. Count Blood had warned him about Sasha. And now it was too late.

He'd have to tell his parents about Count Blood. Maybe they could even go see him. He might be able to help.

Ivan ran into his room and stopped in front of the mirror. He opened his mouth and imagined what he would look like with fangs.

Me . . . a vampire. Ivan wasn't sure how he felt about that. His birthday was six months away. Then he'd know for sure.

"Count Ivan," he said aloud, staring at his reflection. "I like the sound of that!"

THE END

Ivan decided to stay home. Count Blood was probably right. It would be too dangerous. He'd have to settle for reading his comic books tonight.

Ivan turned to walk up the stairs when he heard a voice behind him.

"I'm looking for Count Blood."

Ivan sighed and turned around. "Listen, if you're another vampire hunter—" he began.

A skinny man with scraggly blond hair and a beard stood on Ivan's front walk. He wore wire-rimmed glasses, ripped jeans, and a red T-shirt emblazoned with a yellow skull. Ivan felt goose bumps rise on his arms.

It wasn't a vampire hunter. It was Fang. Ivan recognized him from the comic book.

Ivan slowly backed up the front steps. But Fang quickly moved in front of him. He stared at Ivan, his eyes a pale blue through his glasses. Ivan found himself staring back into Fang's eyes, unable to move.

"I'm no vampire hunter," Fang said. "I think you know what I am."

Ivan nodded, too frightened to speak.

"Word on the street is that Blood is crashing at your pad," he said. "Is that true?"

"He . . . he left last night," Ivan stammered.

"He's not here."

Fang sniffed the air. "No," he said. "Maybe not."

The whole time, Fang kept his eyes locked with Ivan's. Ivan tried to look away, but he couldn't.

"Too bad," Fang continued. "I'd hate to think I've come all this way for nothing."

Ivan stood, frozen, as the vampire absently rubbed his stomach. "I am hungry, though," Fang said.

Fang opened his mouth, revealing two long, sharp fangs. Then he cackled.

"Help!" Ivan tried to scream, but the word came out as a whisper.

He tried to move, but he couldn't. He felt locked to the spot.

And the vampire closed in . . .

THE END

Continued from page 61

Ivan flew to the right. He zigzagged down another tunnel—and then smacked right into a stone wall!

Dazed, Ivan fell to the ground. Then he felt a cold hand grip his body.

"Too bad you didn't get more practice," Fang said, grinning at him. "You might have gotten a hang of that echolocation thing. Lucky for me you're banging into walls."

Ivan wriggled, trying to get out of Fang's grasp. But it was no use. Fang yanked the medallion off of him.

"I'll be taking this," he said. "Of course, you won't be able to change back without it. Tough luck, kid."

Fang let go of Ivan. He fluttered around the vampire in a panic.

"Squeak! Squeak! Squeak!" Give me back the medallion!

Fang laughed. "I've got to split. I hear Blood's headed this way, looking for you. Too bad he won't find you." Fang walked back down the tunnel, then turned. "Good luck with the bat thing!"

Ivan still had hope. If Count Blood was coming, Ivan could warn him—somehow. He'd have to try, anyway. But first he'd have to get out of here.

Ivan flew back down the way he had come, then headed down the tunnel. He hadn't gone far when he smelled something—fresh air.

Ivan made another turn and saw moonlight shining through an opening. He flew through it.

A tall, stone building rose up next to him. Ivan recognized it—the Bleaktown Historical Society. Count Blood had said his headquarters was underneath the society. This must be another entrance.

Then Ivan saw a tall figure walking toward him. Count Blood! Ivan flew to him.

"Squeak! Squeak, squeak, squeak! Squeak, squeak!" *It's me, Ivan! I got turned into a bat! Don't go in there! It's a trap!*

Count Blood stopped and looked at Ivan. For a second, Ivan thought he might recognize him.

"Have you seen my friend Ivan?" Count Blood asked the bat.

"Squeak! Squeak! Squeak!"

"I just hope he is safe," Count Blood said sadly. "I am afraid I may have sent him into danger."

Count Blood continued toward the tunnel entrance. Ivan flapped along behind him, squeaking frantically.

But the count didn't know he was being warned. He stepped through the entrance and then closed the door, almost clipping Ivan's wing. Ivan helplessly hovered outside the door.

Seconds later, he heard scuffling noises, and a cry of surprise from Count Blood. There were more scuffling noises, and finally he heard Fang's evil laugh.

"I've got you now, Blood," Fang crowed. "You'll never escape!"

"*Squeeeeak!*" Ivan cried. But it was no use.

Ivan flew to a tree branch and hung upside down.

Fang had captured Count Blood.

Ivan had been turned into a bat, and he didn't know how to turn back.

"I never should have bought that vial at the junk shop," Ivan wailed. But, of course, all that came out was . . .

"*Squeak!*"

THE END

"Maybe we should try Dr. Mystic's spell first," Ivan suggested. "If it doesn't work, then we can go to Count Blood's coffin."

"All right," Coburn said. "I think I remember it."

"Don't you have issue fifty-seven?" Ivan asked.

"I had to sell off my issues," Coburn said a little sadly. "Times have been tight."

"I've got them all at home," Ivan said. "Why don't we go there? Then we can do the spell exactly."

Coburn looked down at his slippers. "Give me a minute."

They pulled in front of Ivan's house about a half hour later. Nana was stirring a pot on the stove, as usual, as they entered the kitchen. A warm, spicy scent filled the air.

"Nana, this is Dave Coburn. He's a comic-book creator," Ivan said proudly.

"Those books are no good for your brain!" Nana scoffed, not looking up from her pot.

"That smells delicious, ma'am," Coburn said in a charming voice.

Nana looked up. Her expression softened.

"It's goulash," she said. "You like that?"

"My own grandmother made the best,"

Coburn said. "And yours smells just like hers."

Nana beamed. "Sit down. Sit down. I'll fix you a plate."

"I'll go get the book," Ivan said. He ran upstairs.

When he came back down, Coburn was eating a plate of goulash and talking with Nana like they were old friends. Ivan plopped issue fifty-seven in front of him.

"I've got it," he said.

Nana picked up the book. "What is this? You did this?"

Coburn nodded. "A long time ago."

Nana flipped through the pages. "Very exciting. And the pictures are so nice. You draw good."

Ivan couldn't believe it. Nana had never liked his comics before!

Coburn blushed. "I don't do that anymore."

"You should, Davey, you should," Nana gushed. "You are very good."

Just then the phone rang. Nana got up from the table and answered it. She began to talk and took the phone into the other room.

"Let's check out the spell," Ivan said. He looked at the comic book.

The art showed Dr. Mystic, a tall man with dark hair and a beard. He wore a purple suit, and a purple gem glittered in the center of his forehead.

Dr. Mystic was sitting on a blanket in a cemetery. He had a bowl of water, a bowl of salt, and what looked like some kind of root vegetable on the blanket in front of him. He was chanting.

"By the powers of the elements.
Let what has been undone be done.
By the powers of the sea and sky.
Let what has been taken away be restored."

"That looks pretty simple," Ivan said.

"We should do it as close to Count Blood as possible," Coburn suggested. "We'll go to the Bleaktown Historical Society."

Ivan pointed to the vegetable in the picture. "What's that?"

Nana had returned to the room. She looked over his shoulder. "It's a parsnip," she said.

"I thought it was a ginger root," Coburn said.

"Nonsense!" Nana said. She opened up a cabinet, reached inside a wicker basket, and picked out a white vegetable. "Parsnip!"

Ivan picked it up. "Could I borrow this, Nana? I'd like to uh . . . practice drawing it."

"Of course," Nana said. "Drawing a parsnip is a good thing."

Coburn polished off his goulash. He took his plate to the sink and washed it. "Thanks for the goulash, ma'am. It was delicious," he said.

Nana beamed again. "Thank you."

"Nana, can I spend the afternoon with Dave? He's going to teach me about comic books," Ivan said.

"Of course!" Nana enthused. "Davey is a nice boy. You could learn a lot from him."

Coburn blushed. Ivan talked Nana into lending them two bowls and some salt. He got a blanket from the linen closet. Then he and Coburn headed to the Bleaktown Historical Society.

It was after three when they got there, and the society had just closed. Coburn led Ivan to the back of the building. A small cemetery sat there, surrounded by a rickety wooden fence. Old tombstones jutted out of the grass.

"Count Blood's coffin is somewhere under there, hidden in a maze of tunnels," Coburn explained. "But I think if we do the spell up here, we should be close enough."

Ivan nodded. He spread out the blanket on the grass in the middle of the tombstones. He filled one bowl with water from a bottle, and another bowl with salt. He put the parsnip between them, just as Dr. Mystic had done in the picture.

"Are you sure that's a parsnip?" Ivan asked again.

"I can't remember," Coburn said. "But Nana

seemed sure. And if we're wrong, what's the worst that can happen? We can always go out and get a ginger root and try that."

Ivan nodded. He looked at the blanket. "What next?"

"Don't look at me," Coburn said. "You're the one you brought Count Blood back to life. This is your gig, kid."

Ivan knew Coburn was right. He sat cross-legged on the blanket. Then he held the comic book in front of him and began to chant.

"By the powers of the elements.
Let what has been undone be done.
By the powers of the sea and sky.
Let what has been taken away be restored."

Ivan looked around. "How will we know if it works?" he asked.

"I'm not sure," Coburn admitted. "There should be, like, a pop or something. Keep trying."

Ivan said the words a second time. Then a third.

Then the ground beneath them began to shake.

"Did you feel that?" Coburn asked.

Before Ivan could answer, he saw something pushing up from the grass next to the blanket. He scrambled out of the way.

It was a hand—a skeleton hand.

Ivan looked around the cemetery. Skeleton hands were clawing their way out of the ground. Ivan knew their skeleton bodies weren't far behind.

"Maybe we shouldn't have used the parsnip," Coburn joked nervously.

"What are we going to do?" Ivan wailed.

"I don't know," Coburn replied. "Think of something!"

Ivan's mind raced as he thought of every Dr. Mystic comic book he had ever read. Sometimes, Dr. Mystic had to undo some of his spells.

Ivan tried to remember. Backwards . . . sometimes Dr. Mystic read his spells backwards.

And then there was something with salt. Maybe scattering it around? Ivan couldn't remember.

Another skeleton hand popped up at Ivan's feet. He screamed and jumped out of the way.

"We've got to try something!" Coburn yelled.

If Ivan says the spell backwards, go to page 75.

If Ivan scatters the salt, go to page 102.

Continued from page 61

Ivan flew down the left fork. It wasn't long before he smelled fresh air. Ivan followed the smell around another turn and saw moonlight streaming through an opening in the wall.

Ivan flew through the opening into the night. He saw a large, stone building in front of him and recognized it as the Bleaktown Historical Society. Count Blood had said his headquarters was underneath the society. This must be an entrance!

Then Ivan saw a tall figure walking toward him. Count Blood! Ivan flew toward him in an excited frenzy.

"Squeak! Squeak, squeak, squeak! Squeak, squeak!" *It's me, Ivan! Don't go down there! It's a trap!*

Count Blood brushed at the bat with his hand. "Excuse me. But I must find my friend Ivan."

Oh, no! Ivan thought. *He doesn't recognize me.* Ivan flew right in front of Count Blood's face.

"Squeak! Squeak!" *It's me! It's me!*

Count Blood started to brush Ivan away again, but then his eyes narrowed. He reached out and touched the medallion around Ivan's neck. Then he raised his eyebrows.

"Can it be?" he wondered. He looked closely at Ivan. "Ivan? Is that you?"

"Squeak! Squeak!"

"Listen closely," Count Blood said. "The medallion you are vearing has the power to turn the vearer into a bat."

"Squeak!" No kidding!

"To become human again, all you must do is concentrate. Imagine yourself in your human form," Count Blood instructed.

Ivan obeyed. He tried to conjure up a picture of himself in his mind: dark hair, pale skin, glasses. His body began to tingle once again. Seconds later, he realized his feet were touching the ground.

"Cool," Ivan said, and was surprised that it didn't come out as a squeak.

"Now tell me vat has happened," Count Blood said.

Ivan explained how Rose had lured him to Fang, how Fang wanted to set a trap for the count, and how he had escaped and found the secret chamber with the medallion. Count Blood nodded.

"You have done vell," he said. "And now, ve have the upper hand. Let me think."

Minutes later, Count Blood had thought of a plan. He explained it to Ivan.

"I do not vant to put you in any more danger," the count said when he was done. "I vill understand if you refuse."

"I vill do it—I mean, I will do it," Ivan said.

"That guy Fang is rotten. Let's take him down."

Count Blood nodded. "You know vat to do."

Ivan closed his eyes and thought about turning into a bat. His skin began to tingle again, and he clenched his teeth, waiting for the pain he knew would come. His muscles cramped up, and seconds later, he was flapping around Count Blood's head.

Ivan flew back into the tunnel. He tracked his way back to Fang's room. The vampire stood there, fuming and yelling at his crew.

"How could you let that bat get away?" he yelled.

Then he looked up, saw Ivan, and a grin spread across his face.

"Looks like bat boy couldn't find his way out," he said, leaping forward. "I'll get him myself this time!"

Ivan was ready. He flew back the way he had come. Fang was right behind him, but couldn't quite catch him.

Soon Ivan reached the entrance. He flew outside, then hovered a few feet away from the opening.

"Gotcha!" Fang said, springing forward.

"No," said Count Blood. "I have got *you*!"

The count stepped out of the shadows, his arms extended in front of him. White, glowing light shot from his fingertips and enveloped Fang, forming a bubble. The vampire struggled helplessly as the bubble lifted him off the ground.

"No fair!" Fang protested. "You tricked me!"

The left corner of Count Blood's mouth raised into a smile. "Ve are vampires," said the count. "There is no such thing as fair."

The count motioned toward Fang. In an instant, the bubble disappeared—and Fang along with it.

There was a gasp from the tunnel entrance, and Ivan turned to see the tattooed vampire and the rest of Fang's crew standing there.

"Go now," Count Blood ordered in a menacing voice, "or you vill be next."

The vampires didn't hesitate. They weren't so tough without their leader. They charged out of the entrance like rats leaving a sinking ship.

Ivan focused on being human again, and found himself standing next to Count Blood.

"We did it!" Ivan said proudly.

Count Blood nodded. "I could not have done it vithout you, Ivan," the count said. "Thank you."

Go to page 48.

Continued from page 110

Ivan didn't want his night of adventure to end. When Sasha's car was out of sight, he walked down the stairs and headed for the bus stop.

Since his nana didn't drive, Ivan knew the Bleaktown bus system as well as any of the drivers. He caught the bus on the corner of Main Street and took it to the last stop—the bus depot. As Ivan got off, the driver looked strangely at him but didn't say anything.

It was a short walk from the bus depot to the abandoned amusement park. As Ivan walked along the highway, he could see the Ferris wheel up ahead. Tonight, it looked different than usual.

It was lit up—and moving.

Excited, Ivan broke into a run—something he didn't do often. He slowed down to a fast walk. As he got closer, he could make out the burned-out buildings and rides in the shadow of a Ferris wheel. A roller coaster track rose into the sky—and then ended abruptly. The torn-canvas top of a merry-go-round flapped in the breeze. Prize booths with empty and broken shelves were scattered among the rides.

A loud cry pierced the air, and Ivan looked in the direction of the sound. He could see Sasha sitting on top of an old building marked with a

"Fun House" sign. She had her crossbow aimed at a group of vampires who were climbing up the building after her. Ivan guessed they were vampires, anyway. They didn't look friendly.

Ivan didn't know what came into him, but he ran toward Sasha, wanting to help. She saw him coming and scowled. Then she reached into her jacket and threw something in Ivan's direction.

"Use this!" she yelled.

Ivan caught the object—a large, yellow water gun, more like a rifle, really. Seeing Ivan, three of the vampires jumped off the building and headed toward Ivan.

As they came closer, Ivan could see their sharp fangs. The three vamps all wore leather jackets with a yellow skull patch on the right arm. Ivan stood, frozen, not sure what to do.

"Ivan, that's holy water!" Sasha called down.

Something in Ivan's brain clicked, and he lowered the water gun. He aimed it at the attacking vampires and began pumping the handle.

Bam! Bam! Bam! Blasts of water hit each of the vampires, one by one. They howled in pain.

And then they vanished in a puff of smoke.

"Good work, Ivan," Sasha said, climbing down from the Fun House. "I dusted my first vampire when I was twelve."

"I thought you said fighting vampires wasn't

for kids?" Ivan pointed out.

Sasha shrugged. "Not for most kids. I guess you're different."

Ivan looked around. "Where's Count Blood?"

Sasha pointed to the Ferris wheel. "Up there. But he's got to do this one without our help, I think."

Ivan looked up. Count Blood and a skinny vampire were locked in a fighting stance on one of the Ferris wheel carts. The cart moved slowly around the wheel.

"You and I took care of Fang's creeps," Sasha said. "But the count needs to take care of Fang himself."

Ivan gazed up at the battle. White light burst from Count Blood's hands, lighting up the night sky. Fang countered with an assault of red lightning bolts. They parried back and forth. It looked like some kind of mini-fireworks display.

The Ferris wheel cart circled down, close to the ground, and then back up again. When the cart reached the top, Ivan saw a huge explosion of white light and heard a scream. But he couldn't see what happened.

"Do you think he—" Ivan began.

"We'll know soon," Sasha said.

The Ferris wheel cart circled back to the ground. As it got closer, Ivan saw Count Blood—alone.

Sasha ran to the Ferris wheel controls and began pulling levers. The ride groaned to a halt, and Count Blood stepped out of the car.

"Fang is no more," he said simply.

"Good job, Count," Sasha said. "I'm impressed."

"And I am impressed vith you," Count Blood said. "You took care of Fang's minions."

"I had help," Sasha said, pointing to Ivan. "The kid's not bad."

"I thought ve told you to stay home, Ivan," Count Blood said.

"I wanted to help," Ivan said. "Besides, this is the most fun I've ever had in my whole life. Can I go on helping you guys?"

Count Blood and Sasha looked at each other and nodded.

"Very vell, Ivan," Count Blood said. "Ve vould be proud to have you help us fight evil."

Go to page 142.

"It won't take long," Ivan said. "I'd feel safer if we got the comic book."

Coburn sighed. "All right. But I'm going to say I told you so."

They all drove to Ivan's house. He quickly ran inside, got issue eighty-five from his bedroom, and ran back to the car. Ivan flipped through the pages as they drove to the historical society.

Soon he found the panel with Dr. Mystic reciting the spell. Dr. Mystic was a tall man with dark hair and beard. He wore a purple suit, and a purple jewel glittered in the center of his forehead. A bubble came out of his mouth with the words to the spell. They were exactly as Coburn had remembered them.

"Uh, looks like you were right," Ivan said sheepishly.

"I told you so," Coburn grumbled.

Minutes later, the car pulled in front of the Bleaktown Historical Society. They stepped out into the darkness and walked toward the back.

Suddenly, bright lights lit up the night, and a roaring sound filled the air. Ivan squinted to see that they were surrounded by motorcycles. A man stepped off one of the motorcycles and walked toward them. He was tall and skinny, with scraggly blond hair and a beard. He wore a red T-shirt emblazoned with a neon yellow skull.

"Fang?" Ivan whispered. He recognized the vampire from the comic book.

"We've been looking for you, Blood," Fang said. "Who've you got with you? More for our crew?" Fang walked closer, and his expression soured. "Is that what I think it is around your neck? Then I guess our friendship is over."

"You are right," Count Blood replied.

"Get 'em, boys!" Fang yelled.

The motorcycle riders—all vampires—jumped off their bikes. Coburn quickly began the incantation.

"*Depth of sea. Strength of rock*—ooph!"

Three vampires tackled Coburn at once. Ivan turned to Count Blood, but he was grappling one-on-one with Fang.

Ivan tried to run, but didn't get far. Two of the motorcycle vampires knocked him down. Ivan hit the grass with a thud.

He looked up to see two fang-filled faces staring down at him.

"*Heeeeeeeeeelp!*" Ivan screamed.

That was the last thing he remembered.

Ivan woke up in his own bed. The window shade was drawn, but a sliver of morning sunlight snuck through.

The light seemed to burn through Ivan's eyes. He ran over and shut the shade all the way. Then he climbed back in bed.

He felt terrible. His head was pounding, and his throat felt like he had swallowed an old sock. Even his teeth hurt.

What exactly had happened last night? Ivan couldn't remember.

Count Blood must have saved me, Ivan thought. *How else would I be home in my own bed? I don't seem to be hurt.*

Ivan got out of bed again and walked to the mirror, just to be sure. He put on his glasses.

He looked normal, for the most part. Then he noticed something strange on his neck. He leaned in closer.

Two tiny red marks stuck out from his pale skin.

"Could be mosquito bites," Ivan said hopefully.

But as he spoke, Ivan saw two white fangs flash in his mouth. He gasped.

"I've been turned into a vampire!" he cried.

Then the memories came flooding back. Fang, sinking his teeth into Count Blood. Dave Coburn, screaming as he fought vampire after vampire. And then the screams had stopped.

And then Ivan had started screaming. He shuddered at the memory.

So he was a vampire now. And he felt hungry.

Very hungry.

I don't have a medallion like Count Blood, Ivan realized. *What's to stop me from being an evil vampire like Fang?*

Ivan looked in the mirror and grinned.

"Nothing," he said.

Then he threw back his head and laughed.

THE END

Continued from page 137

Sasha and Count Blood drove Ivan home. He got inside just minutes before Nana returned from her night out.

"Hello, Bubby," she said, giving him a kiss. "Did you have fun tonight? What did you do?"

Let's see, Ivan thought. *I got kidnapped by a crazy vampire hunter. I saw a real ghost. I vaporized three vampires with holy water.*

"Not much," Ivan answered.

Nana shook her head. "Reading comic books again, I bet. What a waste of time!"

"Nana, can I go downtown again tomorrow?" Ivan asked. "I want to go back to that junk shop."

"To look for more comic books?" Nana asked.

"Actually, I had something else in mind," Ivan said.

The next morning, Ivan woke up early. He put on his glasses and looked at himself in the mirror.

"Ivan Melchik, vampire hunter," he said in a deep voice. Then he grinned. "Not bad."

Ivan couldn't wait to start battling evil with Sasha and Count Blood. But he wanted to be prepared. He needed gear—special gear. And he guessed that Sebastian Cream's Junk Shop might be just the place to get it.

After a typical one of Nana's big breakfasts,

Ivan headed downtown. When he pushed open the door to the shop, he found a boy kneeling down next to the front door, looking through a box of books. Ivan stepped over the boy and walked up to the counter. Mr. Cream sat on a high stool, peering at Ivan through his glasses.

"Hello," he said. "Did you find the vial to be satisfactory?"

It was an odd question, and Ivan thought about the answer. Was he satisfied with the vial? The events of the last days had definitely been satisfying, even though they'd been scary and weird, too.

"Yes," Ivan answered. "And I'm looking for some new items."

Mr. Cream raised an eyebrow. "I don't usually get repeat customers," he said. "What exactly are you looking for?"

Ivan glanced back at the boy. He leaned over the counter and whispered to Mr. Cream. "It's kind of, uh, confidential."

"Don't worry about him," the shop owner replied. "He's absorbed in his books. He doesn't even know we're here."

Ivan nodded. He had been like that, sometimes, when he was reading his comic books.

"Okay," he said. "I need equipment. For fighting vampires. And monsters."

Mr. Cream looked pleased. "Ah, excellent. I have a large selection."

The shopkeeper walked out from behind the counter and motioned for Ivan to follow him to a corner of the room. He led Ivan to an old, wooden trunk and opened it up.

Ivan leaned over. Inside the trunk were all kinds of strange objects—medallions with strange carvings, bottles of neon-colored liquid. It all looked really cool and interesting.

"Browse a little," said Mr. Cream. "I'd be happy to answer any questions you have."

Ivan smiled and looked at the trunk. He thought of the boy looking at the books and felt sorry for him. Ivan's life was better than any comic book. The boy in the store would never know what that was like.

Then Ivan had a thought. His adventure had started in Sebastian Cream's shop. Maybe this boy had an adventure in store, too.

"Guess he'll find out soon enough," Ivan said. Then he began exploring the trunk.

THE END